SUDDENLY LIGHT

NINA DUNIC

SUDDENLY LIGHT

NINA DUNIC

INVISIBLE PUBLISHING
Halifax | Fredericton | Picton

Library and Archives Canada Cataloguing in Publication

Title: Suddenly light / Nina Dunic. | Names: Dunic, Nina, author.
Identifiers: Canadiana (print) 20250191288 | Canadiana (ebook) 2025019130X | ISBN 9781778430695 (softcover) | ISBN 9781778430701 (EPUB)
Subjects: LCGFT: Short stories.
Classification: LCC PS8607.U537 S83 2025 | DDC C813/.6—dc23

Edited by Bryan Ibeas
Cover and interior design by Megan Fildes
Typeset in Laurentian with thanks to type designer Rod McDonald

The publisher dedicates this book to Matthew Montgomery, a generous reader and friend of the press, who did not live long enough to read it.

Invisible Publishing is committed to protecting our natural environment. As part of our efforts, both the cover and interior of this book are printed on acid-free 100% post-consumer recycled fibres.

Printed and bound in Canada.

Invisible Publishing | Halifax, Fredericton, & Picton
www.invisiblepublishing.com

Published with the generous assistance of the Canada Council for the Arts, the Ontario Arts Council, and the Government of Canada.

Canada Council for the Arts Conseil des Arts du Canada

ONTARIO ARTS COUNCIL
CONSEIL DES ARTS DE L'ONTARIO
an Ontario government agency
un organisme du gouvernement de l'Ontario

Canada

In memory of MM,
a friend of a friend

CARDINAL

IT WAS A STRANGELY SNOWLESS DECEMBER. Derek and I had not seen each other since the summer, spending an afternoon in July on a clean, steel-and-glass patio in midtown, getting a bit drunk but trying to flatten it out with food. We eventually moved to a crowded eastside pub and then a dive bar—our venues growing as sloppy as we were. As usual, by the end, we were suddenly falling into brotherly hugs and talking about things that normally did not appeal to either of us. Our parents, work, women that had disappointed us. Often the same stories. Repetition was not tiresome but soothing, like wheels going round and round. Then french fries, sleep, and he took the train back to Burlington in the morning.

Now it was my turn to visit him. It didn't feel much like Christmas yet without the snow, but I usually went to his place around this time of year. I liked a little bit of snow around, to feel festive. Otherwise the decorations in the shops—and women's pretty little scarves or coloured tights—somehow turned a little sad; their efforts seemed misplaced in a grey city. It was a theme with me, a little bit of prettiness turning lonesome.

Brenda didn't come with me. Derek's apartment—a rented floor in a cold, brick house—was not suited to hosting company, did not have a proper table for a proper meal. More than that, Derek was not suitable company for girlfriends; he did not know how to interact with women he was not interested in. Or any person, for that matter—polite obligations taxed him and, drinking, he would grow snide. Brenda and I never said anything along those lines, about the table or otherwise; I just saw him sometimes and did not extend the invite, and she did not ask to come.

The small train station was warm and crowded on a weekend close to the holidays. A man wearing a coat with a hockey team logo stood holding a sloppily wrapped gift, staring at the wall-mounted board that showed train times. A pale, thin young woman sat nearby, not looking at anything. She seemed twitchy and abandoned, with red around her nostrils—she should have been wearing a hat. A mother in her thirties bustled in, attempting to both soothe and admonish three restless children; there was a hard brightness in her voice intended for the rest of us. But a well-off couple was the warm, glowing centre of the station. They both wore coats with the shoulder patch—indicating they spent on jackets what I once spent on a used car—and both had aviator sunglasses, mirrored. Like twin helicopter pilots. Their lips looked creamy and moisturized, and I admired them for a few minutes; they looked like they would never get old, never get sick.

The train ride was an unremarkable passage through industrial tracts of land and the ugly backs of buildings. Occasionally the train passed a new development, a subdivision of pink and beige townhouses, huddled together, staring at each other through kitchen windows. Who wants a pink house? The brick was probably called "salmon" or "coral"—but it was pink. Burlington. I texted Derek and said I would be landing at quarter after four. He texted, *K.* I fiddled with my phone for a few minutes, cycling through apps but not lingering on anything in particular. Finally I posted, *help, i'm going to burlington.*

Derek seemed to have lost a little weight. I smiled through the passenger-side window and then got in the car. It looked all right on him; he didn't look thin exactly. He looked maybe younger—except the eyes; his eyes looked older. He was wearing a leather bomber jacket over a navy-blue sweatshirt, with trim pants—not jeans—tucked into bulky boots. Handsome guy. He was grinning at me, evidently in a good mood today. I was relieved.

"Heeeeeeeeeeeey Jamesy," he drawled out in an impressive display of older-brother dominance.

"Your car smells like shit," I said, my younger-brother attempt at appearing gruff.

"I can't smell it anymore." He was still smiling as we were pulling out. "I refuse to smell it anymore. I win."

Derek wanted to drive to the bar but I told him we should walk. Park at your house and walk to the bar, I said. He made a theatrical sigh but turned for the house, knowing I was always willing to mention a former girlfriend's younger brother, killed by a drunk driver. Patrick. He was the only dead teen in our high school. It changed our school; we had assemblies about it. It changed my girlfriend. For a long time I thought I would stay with her, take care of her, marry her, to make up for it.

We parked, didn't even step inside the house with my bags, just walked to the bar with our shoulders hunched up and hands stuffed in our pockets. "Cold," Derek said.

"Patrick's colder in the ground," I said. I win.

The waitress brought us a pitcher of beer. In the city you called them servers, but here they were waitresses. There was a female performance aspect. The contours of her smile changed as she looked from me to Derek.

"How's Brenda?" Derek asked, pouring a pint. One question, no follow-up, so I would have to make it count.

"She's good. We're talking about moving in together. She also talks about kids too, which I am thinking about. So we're good; it's serious."

"Ah," he said. "That sounds niiiiiiice, James."

I hadn't mentioned marriage; it was a word that carried some weight between us. "So what happened to Erica, then?" I asked. "The same that always happens?"

"The same," he said, smirking. "She just wanted attention; it didn't necessarily have to be mine."

"Well, you pick them for the same reason, so."

"So," he repeated. He rubbed the side of his face with his palm, his thoughts leaving the room. "Yeah," he concluded.

He was a warehouse manager for a spice importing company. His clothes often smelled vaguely of cumin, coriander, a tickle of pepper. The rest of his life was the gym and hockey, weed and beer. His notebooks, though. His notebooks filled the lowest shelf on his bookcase—mostly the kind of inexpensive "cahiers" that we had used in school. A few of them nicer journals that were purchased for him as gifts, hardcover, a few leather ones with the embossed initials. He filled them, and then they filled the shelf.

"I just write some words when I'm high," he would say. He knew that I wrote a lot for my job—part of my role in marketing—and he knew that other people read my work, commented on it, and even shared it. Once or twice he expressed some admiration, although he never read what I wrote—it was industry stuff, ultimately disposable, even to me.

His work was the same. His boss was okay, but another manager there got on his nerves—"a little prick." The renter that lived upstairs had moved out, and the new renter was a really old guy who was a bit weird, but harmless. At least he was quiet; shifts at the warehouse started at seven a.m. The renter did like animals—birds and squirrels and chipmunks and such—and this seemed like an endearing quality, considering he also walked strangely and sometimes swatted at his own head.

"He doesn't seem to have anyone at all," Derek said, rolling the pint glass between his palms. "If he has a phone, I've never seen him with it. I guess it makes sense—he's crazy. But you'd think he could find another weird person. Seems bad enough to be crazy, but crazy and alone—it's a bit too sad."

"Well, you're sane and alone."

"Yeah, but at least I have a thriving, creative career," he said, deadpan. Then he grinned—picturesque.

I told him my work was getting better. They had hired beneath me so I was able to delegate a lot of menial work—mostly the reporting—and although it wasn't actually a promotion, it felt like one. My building recently updated the gym and sauna but also increased maintenance fees significantly, which I was not happy about. Brenda and I were talking about cohabiting anyway, which meant I would save half on everything. She had a cat, and I showed pictures on my phone; Derek liked cats.

In about two hours, once we started on rye, he would bring up Sam. Sam was The One. Sam got away. Sam was on the internet somewhere, sharing photos of herself, and lots of people liked it. She was the drunk topic for years. He dumped her but regretted it, and she never asked to come back, and he was too proud to ask—so she found someone worthy but less proud, and he found less proud women but not worthy ones. So she had come out on top, and he had lost.

It fractured some fundamental part of Derek. I didn't know whether it was the mistake itself or his inability to right the mistake that hurt him most. I didn't know how much of it was about Sam at all—but his awe, his terror, at his own immovable ego, even under a lifetime's worth of regret. And he was right to be afraid. It was so stupid—and so characteristic of him—to prefer his ego over his own happiness.

I had met Sam; it was apparent why I should be smitten. She was attractive and lively, somehow both direct and elusive at the same time. Alpha female, provocatively dressed, brisk in movement—she seemed quite an important figure to be associated with. She was disapproving, pretty, tough. And it made men feel important, her presence. Derek's kind of woman.

And it was such a Derek fate to be sitting in a pub in Burlington, still talking about how stupid social media was but how a lot of people liked Sam on it, about six years after the last time they spoke.

The year they broke up. During one of my visits, while he was in the bathroom, I pulled out his notebook and flipped through some pages. Most were crammed with short sentences and small sketches, but one page was blank except for a rushed scribble across the top of the page. *She doesn't know who I am.* That was it, on the page. I had a painful tug in my heart for my brother. He didn't see how much time he spent ensuring nobody knew who he was. He expected he could always do that, but that someone would still know.

After midnight, after rye, he was slumped forward on the bar stool. The game was long over and now they were playing clips. "One of these guys liked a photo of Sam," he said, gesturing to the basketball players on the television. I didn't ask about it.

We left the bar after spending several hours watching and talking about sports. We were drunk. Flurries were coming down as we stomped home, not feeling the cold, but our bodies strangely, painfully contracted nevertheless.

"I'm cold, James!" he shouted.

"I'm cold, Derek!" I shouted back.

Snowflakes flew into our eyes and flashes of the sidewalk, my boots, and occasional trees or lampposts, flickered through my vision.

We got back to his place. He showed me the sofa and a pile of blankets. "You're my favourite brother," I said, stupid with relief.

"No, I'm not," he said.

He went to the bathroom to brush his teeth, and I walked over to the bookshelf, the bottom row. I pulled out a recent journal and opened to a page close to the end.

I felt like a scattering of red birds.

I closed the book and lay down on the sofa, pulling the blankets over me and feeling a strange, warm consciousness in my arms, my stomach, my thighs, my feet pushing beneath the cushions, tight muscles uncurling. A scattering.

He came out of the bathroom and walked over to the sofa, standing over my feet. His figure was silhouetted by a light in the hall. "I just want you to know something."

"Okay," I said.

"There is a chance I might kill myself," he said, without emotion. "But I don't want you to be upset, if it happens."

"I won't," I said.

"Okay," he said. "Thanks, bro."

He walked down the hall.

I realized my overnight bag with toothpaste and socks was freezing in the backseat of the car. I reached for my phone and texted Brenda, *goodnight sweet princess*.

/ / /

Derek didn't kill himself. He met a girl named Jessie and they lived together in a comfortable arrangement. He didn't talk about her much, but he'd text her once or twice as an evening progressed.

Brenda and I moved in together, got married a few years later, and had a daughter soon after that. Time started passing quickly. I watched my daughter look at me with eyes that flashed with new understanding, every week, every month. I could see her consciousness flutter and open, like petals on a flower. Derek liked her. Her name was Belle—Annabelle, but we called her Belle.

I knew my brother. Handsome guy. Lone wolf, too proud. Our parents died early and had despised each other, taking great pains to conceal that from us. There was a final and total meaninglessness to their abrupt lives. I felt it too. The strange weight. Mostly at the edges of the night, as things were winding down. I knew what Derek wanted—scared of death and loneliness, the threat was his bravado. Made him feel brave enough to let the night end, alone. Let himself fall asleep, alone. I got it.

/ / /

We were kind of destroyed the next morning. The old man was outside the house, on the front porch. Derek seemed surprised to see him out front and cleared his throat a few times, saying good morning and introducing me quickly. The man was not interested in me but wanted Derek to see the neighbour's tree out front, a young oak. There was a cardinal in it. Its colour was a deep gash in the neighbourhood's grey; it was inexplicable, startling. "It's pretty," Derek said.

FALLS

SPRING WAS COMING. The sun was lingering a little longer in the west, throwing orange light across the fronts of houses. Dogs and children ambled outdoors, unhurried, silhouetted against the sky. The air was warming, smelling of damp earth, becoming clean.

Often I woke around this time, just before dusk. I worked security at a mall, overnight shift, four years now.

Phoenix Falls, an upscale mall about half an hour outside downtown—it pulled a lot of people in on the weekends; it was rare to get good-sized parking lots right off a main thoroughfare. People drove from all corners of the city. They only just built it about six or seven years ago; before that, it was some massive, empty industrial area, a complex of buildings for something they don't make anymore. I thought they might turn it into trendy townhouses and lofts, but they didn't.

It was a nicer area now. People were buying up the small houses around there; many were torn down for new, big builds. There were nicer cars in the driveways and large family vehicles.

Sometimes I drove around a bit, window open a few inches. I drove past the houses after all their lights were off, except for maybe a bedroom at the back of the house—but sometimes there were no lights at all, everyone asleep, or on their phones in bed. It felt good seeing the small homes and imagining the small, warm rooms inside. It made me feel benevolent toward them; I would be awake while they slept.

The main entrance sat at the end of a long four-lane ramp that gently curved around. You felt like you were circling and climbing as you approached the mall. Apparently the structure looked like a bird from above—a blocky kind of bird outline. They were proud of that, featuring it on their website in several photos and using the shape for their logo. But from the ground, it just looked like stores.

I pulled into the lot and saw a black pickup truck that I didn't know—the only car, except for Dan's hatchback and the two dumpers at the back. It was parked close to the entrance. That must be Mike. I looked at my phone—nothing.

Mike was the new guy; he'd started after the last one left to go work for his brother's business. There was high turnover on the shift. That was my intention as well—this was meant to be a temporary job, an empty and quiet break until something else—but somehow I ended up seeing more new guys come and go than I thought I would. Time was getting away from me. I got out of the car and walked toward him; Mike was standing close to the building.

"Hey man," he said to me. He was a very tall white guy, at least four or five inches over six feet—even his head was tall. He was muscular, though, big—not skinny-tall. Gym guy.

"Hey, you must be Mike," I said.

"Yeah, that's right." He tapped out his cigarette against one of the planters and put away his phone. He put the butt politely in the ash can to his left. He had a deep voice.

"I'm Tav," I said, a nickname the kids had used since childhood. We shook hands.

Mike carried a large gym bag, which he should have left in his truck—a backpack at most—but I didn't say anything. He wasn't wearing the uniform under his jacket either. I texted Dan, who was inside, finishing his shift.

"So," I said to Mike, putting away my phone. "Day 1. Are you ready?"

"Hah, yeah," he said, a bit unsure.

"It's boring, don't get too excited."

He was a big, laid-back dude—with a black pickup, of course—the kind I had worked with before. Aggressively athletic, took care of his body, probably not much to say. A quiet and reliable mind. He'd stay a little more than six to eight months on the night shift, a couple seasons, not a full year.

Then there would be a new Mike, or worse. A weird little guy like Brandon, the last one. Brandon spent a lot of the slow hours taking photos of jewellery and thousand-dollar coats, sending them to his girlfriend as they approached their first anniversary—I guess to get her excited about the possibility of gifts—only to then dump her on the day, confronting her with screengrabs of evidence of her flirting with two other guys. It was a big production for him, a coup. He relished it.

At first I laughed with him, kind of uncomfortable, but later, driving home, I thought there was something really wrong with Brandon. He seemed to have a lot of similar stories. Always after the same types of girls and then always jealous of everything. I thought maybe he despised women and kept finding the same type of woman he could despise, so he could be right. As I drove through brightly lit intersections on empty streets, I couldn't see why he would spend years on it. I felt I only had energy for one or two big disappointments, and after that, I would stop trying.

Not Mike, though. I could tell, physically, he would not be petty, exacting. He had a careless expansiveness, could not find the energy to examine the details—he had the generosity of complete ease. And for that reason, like a law of nature, everything would flow easily toward him. Like a valley that fills with water.

He was probably here for one or more of the following reasons: $23 an hour; easier than construction but better pay than warehouse work; the uniform, suggesting authority; it was a "masculine" role; he had nothing else right now. There were no other reasons, not for a guy like Mike.

And then there was me, driving around at night. Sleeping in a basement apartment with two small windows and heavy blackout curtains—night shift.

Dan came to the south entrance and opened the doors for us. He had let Arjun out already, near his car at the front of the building. We exchanged *heys* and swapped positions—inside for outside. Mike and Dan nodded at each other without saying much.

Mike set his gym bag down on a bench and looked up, looked around, taking a moment. The mall soared two levels above us and dove two levels below for the food court and smaller services shops—its belly was carved out in the centre, so you could see everything, marvel at its insides. The four-storey waterfall was turned off, but it was made mostly of glass and filled with pools of still water. It glittered—water off glass, glass off water, water off glass again. Installations hung from the pitched glass ceiling, wire-suspended human figures cast in a mirrored metal, bending in various languid poses, suggesting I don't know what—maybe that life was easy and beautiful. Something calming to look at between the crowded colours of stores. I'm certain they paid the artist a lot; it looked like the kind of art made for rich people.

"You haven't been in here before?" I asked.

"I live in West Hill," he said. "I don't drive out to this end very often."

He faced me, waiting. I explained night shift to him, the rough outline, where each of us should start, which paths we should take, where we should eat, how to communicate. Where he could change into his uniform. We could do the same levels together to start, so we would pass frequently, but later we would do different levels.

Then I told him about the big heist a few years back, before I started, when the place was new, and how the guys had missed it. Mike perked up right away, asking questions, trying to picture the burglary like a Hollywood movie—a caper. They went for the jewellery and phones, small high-value items, of course. The bad guys were clever and cunning—working against the established order of things, in which all of us obediently participate, without thought—and the good guys were lazy or unsuspecting, lacking the imagination to even be wary. It was all very entertaining. No arrests were ever made.

"Let's walk for a bit together," I said, "and I'll show you the shops."

Jewellery stores, clothing, shoes, electronics, electronic accessories, jeans, a whole store for jeans, sporting goods, home decor, books and music, rugs and lamps, health products, pets—how they clustered together or avoided each other, like an active ecosystem. There was a store that just sold socks. Endless rows of coloured and patterned socks. Even an art gallery—where prices were just barely but precisely attainable—filled with bright canvases, abstract and likeable. I imagined they only needed to sell one or two things a week and the rest of the time they could just look calmly outside, watching the retail masses drifting by. They only needed a tiny fraction of this population to care about them—how liberating. Other retailers fought like dogs to sell phone cases or patterned water bottles, especially on the lower floors. Some disappeared within a year. And that was generally how it worked: the lower floors were cheaper goods; the upper levels were where you bought into the luxury lifestyle—literally in the sky.

You didn't have to be rich to shop on the upper floors. You just had to buy one rich thing, once or twice a year, to walk in the world with these tiny badges of worth—the logo, the brand, the public-facing investment. Everybody on the top floor was still trying. I didn't know where I was, probably on the middle floors and going down.

Mike didn't speak much, so I mostly kept to the script. "Time to change," I said, motioning to the men's room behind him. "Let's cross paths in about an hour. We can do a coffee run halfway through the night. If you see something, say something."

I was being funny, but he nodded seriously. The weight of responsibility was settling on him now—we were here to save the jewellery, the socks, the phone cases, the things that made people happy and calm. I didn't say this out loud; Mike was a big, easy guy, and there was no point confusing him. He would have plenty of time to think about it, if he wanted to.

Time alone.

I walked slowly down the east wing—literally a wing of the bird shape—looking into the stores behind the grating doors. I looked for movement, unfocusing my eyes like I'd read about, before slowly moving on again. Occasionally I looked at my phone—nothing.

Good old Mike. This would be exciting for a while, as he learned the routines and eventually got key access—which we could not use anyway without a report to management since there were sensors on the grates. But it would thrill him, a little, the jangle of keys. And then nothing would happen for weeks and months, and after a couple seasons had passed, he would become bored. It would dawn on him that, likely, nothing would ever happen. And then he would have a cousin or friend somewhere in another company, and he would join them there. And I would say, "Take it easy, Mike." And he would say, "See you around, Tav." Easy come, easy go. The criss-crossing paths of semi-strangers. I pictured a gathering of us, former coworkers, old classmates, distant friends whose lives I vaguely knew online. Full auditoriums of semi-strangers, so many of us, everywhere.

I put in one earbud for a little music. It wasn't allowed, but it was discreet and easy to pull out when I would see Mike coming. It made the night better, letting the thoughts roll out. "Starin' Through My Rear View."

Jewellery stores. People died in those mines. But we kept sending men down there. I even liked jewellery—at least it lasted forever; so much of everything else didn't. I had worn a chain on my chest since I was fourteen years old. Standing in the shower, or after, in the mirror, it was a slim, pale, curved line cutting across the colour of my skin, a delicate detail on my body. Usually I felt strong, tightly packed, tightly wound, but big guys like Mike reminded me about real power—he was probably two heads taller than me. It commanded a different world around him, with other men, with women—I could only imagine the women in his phone—and I'd always known that world was not my own. And for Mike, he didn't even know. I would compare myself to him but he would not compare himself to me. I had known so many careless Mikes all my life, watched them move through the world—effortless, like big, languid cats, sleeping in the sun.

But it didn't matter as much anymore. I was removing myself from the world, slowly collecting the parts of me that were exposed. Working at night, living alone, deciding how and when I wanted to come back. "XO Tour Llif3."

I saw Mike walking toward me; I slipped the earbud out. His posture looked a little aimless until he saw me, then he perked up, mobilized the security-guard shoulders. He had walked a little too quickly through his portion, but that was a common thing to start. He seemed like a basically nice guy, trying to do a good job.

"Fun, right?" I said.

"Yeah," he said. "Good so far."

"Have you seen the big face yet?" I asked. "On the floor."

"Oh yeah, on the floor," he said. "I saw that."

"And if you look up, there's a glass panel on the ceiling, which is the floor on the level above us." I was gesturing. "So you can see it from one level up, too, through the glass."

I was more interested in describing it to Mike than Mike was interested in hearing about it. But he was nice about it, nodding with me.

We moved to the second level, separating, starting the rounds together from opposite ends. I went to the glass panel and stood over it, looking down.

It was an ad for perfume. A model was lying on a beach—delicate grains of sand clung to the contours of her neck, the lobes of her ears, her fingertips, which were held close to her mouth—and she was looking at you. Her face was more than sixty feet across, on the floor of the first level. It was like a billboard lying on the ground.

The model was cast in bronze—face, arms, neck. Smooth as polished metal, her face was a perfect oval with nude lips in the middle, a gentle pink within the bronze. And the eyes—an absolute crystalline turquoise, the colour you see in postcards, when beaches are shallow on white sand.

She wasn't real. I knew that. It wasn't about whether or not her eyes were that colour, whether they sprayed the bronze on her skin or lacquered it with a computer program. It was how alien it made me feel. Too far from everything else in the world.

It wasn't anything else but that. I was twelve years old with my parents, downtown in a 24-hour diner, and I used the bathroom by myself, and two men in there talked about a sex worker they had paid for; they insulted her. They were still drunk. I came back to the table and my pancakes had arrived. My parents were smiling, watching me. That moment.

And turquoise eyes. Large enough that, if I lay down, they would have been as long as me. Pupils like a black hole where a man could disappear.

Every shift I stood over that image. She was on a beach selling perfume for $190 an ounce. I worked in an empty mall. It was overwhelming—the billboard size of the image, me standing small above it, me remembering that moment in the diner, small again, a child—the impassable space between worlds. It seemed to break whatever understanding, all my life, I had felt but not known, not with any kind of words. That wide separation, that void. The world was far apart in ways we didn't talk about, and all our lives were disappearing in strange currents—and we were hardly making a sound. We were not saying anything about it. It was too big to say.

/ / /

This was better than my first two jobs. My first job was at a gym. I was supposed to clean and care for the equipment and, when people talked to me, try to get them to purchase more services and classes. I would get a commission each time they did. It was fine for a while, about six months to a year, and then somehow it became embarrassing that I was doing this. People were paying to go to a room to exercise with other people around, walls of mirrors, using elaborate machines. I was trying to get them to buy the branded bags and bottles. If someone bought a towel or robe, it was a big deal. Or classes—gathering in a room with loud music and one person yelling at them. Full-time, it was a weird world. And yet I wasn't quite sure what other people were doing, either. I didn't stay in school long enough to get an office job but I suspected those jobs wouldn't have been better. I didn't want to sit at a desk—passing the time, every few years, by moving to a new desk.

The gym was owned by an overweight white guy who dressed poorly and often seemed distressed about some issue or another. He was on the phone a lot. I think his parents had a car business just outside the city, so he was a vaguely rich kid—later they gave him money to buy a business, so he bought a gym. A manager had told me all that. The owner's appearance made it clear he had no interest in health or fitness—I hoped he didn't have cameras in the change rooms, because it seemed possible he was that kind of guy.

He was rude and skimped the employees on hours, so turnover was high. Some people stayed because they didn't think they would find anything better. Some of them liked working out for free, being in the world. I was fit, but I was never interested in getting big. So I left and worked at a car rental place.

The car rental place was interesting for a while—like the gym, I didn't mind it at first. I liked driving and getting in and out of cars, handling keys, helping people. It was simple and satisfying to me. But nobody bought the franchise. It was owned by the corporate head office, and they kept coming up with these numbers that said we weren't efficient enough. And so they understaffed and took away paid breaks, started deducting a half hour for lunch. And on weekends you ate standing up because it was so busy when they staffed three guys instead of four. Our manager was short and balding and trying very hard. I felt as if he grew shorter and lost more hair trying to make corporate accept the efficiency figures, while also telling us what slack we would be cutting this month—trying to look at our faces but not often succeeding. His voice broke a lot, and his ties looked cheap. I pitied the guy; he would ruin himself slowly and not make very much money for it, either. My father had first shown me that.

I don't know what I was expecting. I was okay with a job until it became clear that we were expendable and they were willing to make it as hard as possible to stay with them—just short of everyone deciding to quit at the same time. Just short of that, they were going to make it hard.

So I tucked that away, got the security job at a mall. And I didn't mind it for a couple of years—people left me alone, it was quiet, my manager was a nice guy who had been a guard before so he knew what it was about. They didn't jerk you around. It seemed to me that everybody should operate like that—we would trade the work for money, and neither side would screw the other—but they didn't, almost everywhere you went. Either they wouldn't or they couldn't.

And I was okay with this—walking along empty halls, guarding closed stores. There would never be another heist. We were a deterrent only, here to call the police in case something happened. The uniform gave it formality, the paycheque was good—it was okay.

But there was a choking feeling, gripping me occasionally, shaking me like a dog. What if this continued indefinitely, what if I was always in the basement apartment, always on nights, not finding a better way to make money, what if I turned forty here—they were not questions; they were walls closing in. Almost none of that seemed fathomable, but the possibility caught me sometimes—would I be fifty and grey and see the billboard on the floor—and I could barely breathe.

It came and went in waves.

No one really bothered me here; they didn't try to crush something out of you. I knew girls but not the kind of girls I wanted to know. If I was making better money, maybe—if I was working days. But I had time to think, hide out, decide when and how to come back.

The feeling came and went.

///

I walked along the shops, feeling light. Loose-limbed. Disconnected from things, as if I were floating above. I wasn't feeling down at all. I had been through a down period, and perhaps now it was lifting.

"There's a backpack here," Mike radioed, animated.

"That's my backpack," I said.

"Okay."

So he had made it back around to the benches outside the administrative offices.

We did the third level next and then went down to the lower floor. It was a good time to eat. Tonight we could eat together but typically our breaks would be staggered, I explained. I didn't bring a meal, just oranges. Mike pulled a long sandwich out of his gym bag—it looked like a stick of French bread with meat jammed in there. And a bottle of vitamin water. Not bad. We were sitting in the food court, phones out.

"So, Day 1, halftime," I said. "Having fun?"

"Yeah, it's good," he said, affable, looking through his phone.

"Any questions?"

"Not yet," Mike said. "This is actually my first security job, so I guess I'm starting from the beginning."

"Yeah, it was mine too. Dan, who did the earlier shift, had worked in other places—I think an office building downtown—but he says it's good here, quiet." I was peeling an orange, collecting the peel in little piles.

We didn't say anything for a few minutes. He was eating. I checked the news on my phone: *140 dead in Yemen strikes*.

"It's a nice mall," Mike said.

"Yeah." I turned the phone over. "But I wouldn't shop here." I had come once, during the day, and it was crowded.

It was hard to get parking, and once inside, there were entire families—from grandparents to little children—roaming aimlessly in the department stores, down the corridors, along the shops. Whole families. I paused, considered something humorous for him. "Around the holidays, with the sales, they have overnight stocking and cleaning staff. You'll see them. Things are literally pulled off the shelves, boxes ripped open—it's chaos, a war zone. Everything's all over the ground."

But he was typing into his phone. I ate my orange two segments at a time and then peeled another. I preferred to eat a light meal before work and a big meal after. In between, just oranges. As cold as I could keep them, in a small insulated bag.

Mike finished with his phone, picked up his sandwich log again. I was taking my time with my second orange, contemplating the segments individually. I was trying to think about something, but Mike's large, quiet presence blotted out my thoughts. It occurred to me that I felt self-conscious, and I examined that briefly, turning it around in my mind. Why?

"So how did you get this job?" I asked.

"A friend of mine from high school did security for two years, said it was pretty good," he said. "I took the course. It was expensive, but the starting rate was good."

"Yep, sounds about right," I said. "That pretty much—"

There was a sharp racket, something metallic and scraping, suddenly to our right. We both jerked toward the sound.

We stared. "Did—"

A small, lean figure jumped up from behind a four-foot planter and started running away from us. A short shag of hair bounced wildly from his head as he ran fast—hard.

"Fuck!" I said.

We both jumped up, the chairs clattering to the ground. We took off after him. I was lean, fast, but the small figure tore through the corridor on tiny feet, pounding hard. He was almost gaining distance on us. I whipped my legs ahead of each other, fire shooting through my thighs, arms going. Mike was too big, slow, dropping behind me.

Suddenly Mike fell back—stopped running—and the bottle of vitamin water soared past me. It struck the man in the back of the head, making a loud crack. He fell down, brutally, limp.

I skidded to a stop. I turned to look at Mike, his face was blank and pale. "The fuck did you do?" Mike opened his mouth to say something. But he didn't say anything.

We jogged up to the small body and its twisted limbs. It wasn't a man; it was that homeless woman. She had done this before, hid somewhere, ran around in here at night, doing who knows what. Last year? A year and a half? Her hair had been long then. I stood over her body, lying twisted, somewhat on her side, her leg out. I leaned down and saw the flutter of her eyelids in the deep pockets of her face; she was hollowed-out skinny. Her lips were slightly pulled apart and there was a brown smear close to her mouth. I touched her shoulder and pulled it back gently, so her torso rolled to face up. She started blinking. I smelled alcohol.

"Hey," I said. "Hey."

Mike was standing above us.

She blinked and looked at me, her eyes focused on my face and then Mike's. "What," she started to say and struggled to sit up. I kept my hand on her shoulder.

"You fell down," I said.

"Let go." She tried to pull her shoulder from me. I gripped her upper arm.

"Ma'am, hold on. We have to call the police."

She wrenched her arm from me and tried to crawl away; I grabbed her again. She lashed out, her skinny leg striking me in the ankle. I cursed and grabbed her arm, hard, starting to pull her body to stand up. She kept twisting her torso, kicking her legs out. Adrenalin cauterized into anger inside me. I grabbed her other arm, almost shook her. Hot anger crept up into my chest, neck, face.

"Stop—stop," I stammered.

She kept writhing.

I gripped her arms and squeezed them hard together, trying to hurt her. She cried out in pain.

"Hey," Mike said, reaching for us.

"She won't—" I started but was unable to say. I was hurting her. My mind was hot, crowded; all I could see was the brown smear near her mouth, her face wincing and closed, like a cratered rock. I could smell the alcohol. I felt angry. I hated this part, the physical confrontation; my mind spun around it, spiralled down, hard. Why were we both here? Locked in this stupid moment? Why would she get drunk, hide in a mall? Why was I here? We both should have been somewhere else. Not locked together in this violent, vulgar meaninglessness. She was fighting me, and I was hurting her.

Disgusted with everything, I let her go.

She staggered back, surprised, unbalanced. She stumbled and started to fall. Mike stepped forward quickly and caught her arm. "Miss," he said.

She looked at him suddenly, as if seeing him for the first time. Mike was almost double her height and weight, like a giant holding a child. Her face grew fearful.

"I'm not going to suck your dick!" she shouted.

"Jesus," Mike said softly.

I turned away from them, could not look at her. I radioed for police. "Fucking Dan," I said, to no one. "It's his job to close, get everybody out."

"Let me go," she said, whimpering.

"Ma'am, we are waiting for the police," Mike said quietly.

"Okay. Then let me sit down." She slowly lowered to the floor and sat beside Mike's shoes, drawing her arms around her knees, resting her face on her arm. Mike was looking down at her, something inscrutable in his face.

"Fucking Dan."

/ / /

She vomited when the police arrived. Better than in the cruiser. Drunk tank, trespassing. We didn't say anything about the bottle of vitamin water. It was nonsense, that Mike would have run with it and then thrown it. She didn't know what had happened either. We said she had tripped.

I called my supervisor and asked to go home. After a physical confrontation, we were usually allowed to go home—we would file a report, take the rest of the night off. But I knew it wasn't possible.

"Tav," Peter said, gently, "I can't let you go home with a new guy there. Can't leave him alone."

Something in me felt bruised. All I could see was that brown smear near her mouth. And turquoise eyes. Smelling the alcohol. I could feel it, going into the tunnel, my mind spinning around the images, the shame and disgust. Remembering my grip on her arms, hurting her, wanting to shake her, hard, so she would stop being drunk—wipe her face, so she would participate like the rest of us. Participate, like all of us. Didn't she get it? We didn't want to be here either. Somewhere between the turquoise eyes and the brown smear were the rest of us.

"You okay?" Mike asked.

"Yeah, I'm okay. Just got angry," I said. "Just doesn't make any sense."

Mike didn't ask what.

The sky was getting pale as morning approached. There were two hours left in the shift.

AWAKE

I HAD BEEN GOING THROUGH a stretch of insomnia so I'd taken to sitting up during the night, smoking cigarettes by the window and flipping through old photo albums. I actually quit smoking many years ago but I bought a pack after the third night. And they weren't my photo albums; they belonged to my parents—heavy books with plastic surfaces on the hardboard pages. The photos started as yellowed black-and-whites but later had a faded colour, like the '70s. I had no idea why I had them, but I'd helped them move twice—the albums must have made their way here by accident. When I found out, I didn't give them back.

I didn't start with the photo albums. I started with art books from university: beautiful, heavy, richly coloured volumes that were hard to throw away after school. I looked at Gauguin, Rouault, Matisse, Dufy, and others. I must have been studying French art, though now I remembered nothing. The colours were intriguing, even when they looked rough or poorly assembled. Sitting up through the late hours, turning into early hours, the scenes were otherworldly. And what strange lives—painters standing by rivers, studying light, studying women, models or lovers or sex workers, sometimes maids or young girls, poverty and disease all around them—giants of an era and dying early of pathetic illnesses. Sometimes alcoholism or madness, or TB. Some lived longer, but can you imagine the browned teeth and greasy dishes forgotten throughout the flat? The stained linens? Fine art. Yet all their work was beautiful, sometimes in odd or misleading ways. A chair sitting next to an open window—meaningless scenes made beloved because someone was willing to look for a long time.

The big books had other pleasures. Their weight and smell, the soft gloss of the thick pages. The collected effort of so many others who made such books and how much we paid to own them, the earnest belief we had to eternalize it. Everybody in here was long dead. Not only the artists but the girls too, the women and figures in every frame. Disappeared lives lost to time; generations later I lingered over their outlines on canvas. But I did not worship artists. I already saw too much in life to wait for art to reveal it.

After the art books, I started on the photo albums, bringing a thick stack up the stairs with me and going through them slowly. I smoked cigarettes and turned the big pages. My parents' world was otherworldly, too, though perfectly ordinary—sitting in heavy books, faded and decolourized, as if someone had already decided what their lives meant and was curating its emotions. Late in the albums, I appeared in the pictures with a head of curls, and I studied these images closely. But then I went back to the beginning and started again.

My father, moustached, snug pants. His round face was not handsome. Later, a beard—then clean-shaven for a long time. He truly had a favourite sweater for a significant stretch of his youth—it was brown, with a rounded collar and ribbed hem at the wrist and bottom. Exceptionally dull actually, but there it was, in so many photos. Even after the moustache was gone and through the beard phase. The pants varied, but it seemed he preferred slacks over denim. Wearing shorts, his legs were thin and sensitive-looking, and his right foot would turn in slightly. He was self-conscious. He wore glasses but did not change his frames over several decades.

There he was—standing in front of cars during road trips, sitting on a rock in a forest, sitting on a rock near a river, wearing sunglasses, sometimes looking at the camera and sometimes not. Born Samuel but called Sam his whole life.

And separately, parallel, my mother growing up. She was the one with the mischief in her eye, the wry mouth. She wore snug skirts and billowy blouses, and in her pose it seemed she was a little overly aware of her figure, although it wasn't bad at all, perhaps just a bit wider than most of her friends'. But young women want to be just like their friends—no more, no less. Still her lively face, I thought, made her interesting. She had a stubbornness in her eyes, good-humoured and unafraid.

Her hair started light brown but darkened as she got older, before the abrupt turn to grey. She didn't follow trends—once her skirts turned to slacks, that was that. Her slacks were slim, and her sweaters were long tunics down to the upper thigh, her small shoes brown or black. She was not flashy, but those scrunched eyes and the wry mouth—she stood apart.

Then the photos would start of them together. Posing and smiling. He was shy and seemed to feel undeserving; she felt the moment of having a camera turned on them was silly but worth humouring. A moment, a click—in the book forever.

I admit they looked happy together.

And they were still together, actually. They lived in a condo on the second floor of a mid-rise building about forty minutes away. They moved to an area where there was also a large nursing home—overall, it was a retirement community. It was quiet and there were amenities around. Almost all the traffic around there was older people and their adult children visiting them on Sundays. There was no crime—people were dying regularly of course, but from old age. In fact more people probably died in that neighbourhood than anywhere else in the city.

That's where I met Ed.

/ / /

I got over the insomnia after about a month. It wouldn't last all night anyway, only most of the night, and there would be some time that I slept deeply, two or three hours at a time. It wasn't so bad the next day.

It was an episode. They were not so common, but their cause or purpose was unclear. My life was uncomplicated; I had structured it that way after an awkward, self-conscious youth. I usually spent the first few nights just wondering why I couldn't sleep, but eventually I would get out of bed to spend time with the books. It is odd what can come out of slowness, looking around, thinking about what to think about.

He owned the convenience store in the area. I didn't know his name, but I decided to call him Ed because his head was squarish and his hair was grey-white, like that actor, even though he didn't look much like him otherwise.

He didn't pay attention to you in the store. He picked up and studied the newspaper when you walked in—not out of arrogance, necessarily. It could have been shyness, although he did not reveal that either. He was attentive when you came to the counter, brisk and smiling easily. He often wore plain white t-shirts with nothing on them. They were kept bright and clean.

Ed wasn't fully real to me at first. He never offered himself for consideration in our small exchanges; he was a private man. When I visited my parents, one of my mother's favourite things was to ask me to go to the convenience store and pick up some gum for her. She loved peppermint and chewed enthusiastically, grinning, daring me to admit that my dad was going deaf—and now she could do this whenever she wanted. She had quit smoking decades ago, then quit gum because it annoyed him. But this was her world now—that was what the gum and the grinning meant. So I would see Ed every so often, buying a pack of peppermint.

I had never given him much thought until the day I walked in to buy the gum again and his face—the eyes and the mouth—was bruised. The skin was broken and split in one area, a red line of dried blood. I was taken aback and did not look him in the eye. He was already familiar with this, standing very upright, his back hard, and all of his movements around the cash register were hard and fast—get it out, get it out. I left quickly. And then for the rest of the afternoon, I sat in front of my mother, in a bright mood and chatting freely, circulating around their living room and dusting little shelf objects with a disposable cloth, picking them up and turning them, enjoying their shapes.

"What happened to the guy who owns the convenience store?" I asked.

"I don't know. What do you mean?" she asked.

"Have you been recently?"

"No, I guess not. Not since, maybe, a week ago? Right?" She turned to look at my father.

My father was in the kitchen, crouched down and watching a piece of bread toasting in the oven. They did not own a toaster—he said they were fire hazards. He had obliterated fire hazards from their condo years ago. He did not answer, did not register the question directed at him.

My mother turned back to me. "Why? What happened?"

I realized if I said his face was bruised and disfigured, she would go there tomorrow. She would walk into the store with purpose but also hesitation, self-conscious, and actively look for him and then abruptly look away, having taken in the scene and catalogued a few small details that would be relayed later to several people. The sort of thing any curious and slightly bored person would do. I remembered him working the cash register. I felt the movement of his arms and knew that the air around him was now coloured by something he could not bear—but it was not his choice; it was his circumstance, and so he would bear it with the minimum that was required. But absolutely nothing more.

"I don't know, probably nothing," I said. I knew already I had lost the chance to spare him. She would go tomorrow.

///

The bouts of insomnia did not necessarily surprise me.

At first, I spent some time trying to figure them out, thinking they were clues to a bigger understanding I would reach about myself. But I never felt shocked or unprepared. I think there was a knowledge that at some point in my life, my thoughts would crowd inward until sleep did not come easily. It was a reality that approached slowly and without disturbance.

I must have gone through the photo albums three times each, more slowly on the subsequent reviews, lingering over the pages. I especially scrutinized the photos in which I appeared, always looking for my own face, seeing my parents in me and myself in them. I looked for eyes, mouths, expressions. Was I a happy child? I only remembered myself as blank and watching. Growing up I didn't know who I was; I felt that for a long time. I mixed in with other children, moved in circles of friends, waiting to know. Once I saw a video of myself in high school, laughing loudly and slapping a friend's arm—I didn't recognize that person at all.

And when I saw Ed's bruised face—and my mother never explained, and I never brought it up again—it seemed the most alive and unspoken thing at that time, during the insomnia. Someone had attacked him and hurt him. His face would heal, but I would not be able to forget that stiff self-consciousness, the shame almost, of being seen that way—hurt. Some did not enjoy being seen at all.

/ / /

The Shopkeeper. 1938. Oil on canvas. Someone could have painted Ed sitting among the bright colours of chips and candy bars. An upright man in a white shirt with dark bruises on his face. Or later, after the bruises, a gentle scar around his mouth. In southern Europe, there would be deep Mediterranean sun slanting through the window, broken by flickers of shadow from the leaves of a tree outside. The painter would find order in line and colour among the stacks and shelves, and labour over his hand resting on the counter, the big-knuckled fingers.

Paid—attention was paid. *We pay attention.* That was how we phrased it; I wondered how it translated in other languages, the subtler meaning beneath the words. The artists paid attention to their objects, their scenes or women; the artists spent the time—spent, because time was currency too—and we had these art books, while millionaires bought and sold the originals. My mother built books of her own life, and I sat with them, with an excess of time and attention, spending it and paying it, perhaps the last and only one to do so. And what were the pictures themselves? So much of the same. Histories of disappearing moments. But I was no artist; I did not claim their lives or beauty or fleeting revelations under my name; I was only alone in the night, thinking.

Ed did not ask for attention. He spoke with an accent so he was not born here; he must have spent a lot of money to move and open a store. I thought about leaving a country where I was born to go live and work in another country—what those first years were like, and then the later years, when growing older, when there was time to reflect. I wondered what all those years were like.

He was a compact man; his height was middling and he had that squarish head. His forearms were bulky—maybe he was in the military as a younger man, or maybe he was an athlete. Maybe he liked to work out, although that pastime was sometimes accompanied with a personality he did not seem to have. I remember feeling that he was politely distant, always professional, but that somehow he was watching and taking care of you. I imagined that other people felt that as well. Ed would snap that newspaper briskly when he saw you approaching the cash register; despite how casual he had looked, he had been waiting for you. He was dutiful, silent, proud.

And then one day it had happened. Maybe someone or some people went into the store—maybe they had bad intentions, there was a plan, or maybe they were very drunk and there was a quick grab, an altercation where everybody was confused and it happened very fast. Or it happened at home. It didn't matter where it had been or with who; any of it would be bad. Someone, or some people, had hurt him. And I knew he was not the type for whom being hurt meant nothing.

/ / /

I would have looked at anyone's photo albums. A permanent book of anyone's life. I would spend my life thinking about people that never thought about me. That was one thing I realized while I couldn't sleep.

I would be around, staring from corners, understanding, struggling to, absorbing people's experiences as my own. That time, at a party, I saw a man actively ignoring his wife. The mother ignoring her child. The unloved dog in the neighbourhood that sat in the backyard all the time, never inside. A girl at school born with a deformity in her arms—her presence at school, on the periphery of our lives, but never part of them. All of those things happened to me, somehow. The first time I saw a fight. An accident. A squirrel dragging its hind legs, broken. My mother angry and crying. Memories—most of them were about other people. And somehow the collective assembly of those things was who I was. It would not have occurred to me if I didn't have the insomnia. When I was younger I wandered overseas like everybody else, and my thoughts stayed with the man who sold fruit to the tourists, all day, all year, the sun-leathered skin of his life.

And then these were the nights. I disliked smoking and yet, if I could not sleep, opening a window and lighting a cigarette was an opportunity for me. A five-minute road I could walk down. Smoking—an artifact from someone else's time.

What had happened to Ed? He looked poorer and poorer as time went on. It seemed he was not recovering from the burglary or assault, whatever it had been. Over the next few months and then as winter started, he seemed to be losing weight. Sometimes he read the newspaper, but sometimes he didn't—there were times that you entered the store and he was merely standing there, behind the counter, rigid and odd.

I wondered how the pity would have felt to him, a proud man. Like missing skin and having a bright light shone on you. I pitied him, as anyone would, but I pitied him not just for the attack, but from the pity itself that everyone else poured upon him—a sickly tar. Every single person had seen the violence right there on his face, busted and startling for weeks, then remembered for years. Pity destroys the proud. It was cloying, and ruthless.

Ed was still thin after the winter, into spring. His face had healed but he hadn't regained the weight—and his demeanour hadn't changed; he was still blank and rigid. He was never talkative before, nor had he smiled very often, but he had moved with purpose. Official in his small interactions. But Ed was still injured, somehow. And it was going to last.

He was there for another year, and then he closed the store and someone else opened another one in its place. It was much newer. The new guy behind the counter wore a name tag and had a different accent. He was very cheerful, a tall and lean man with a closely cropped goatee. He enjoyed chit-chat. My parents lived for almost eighteen years in that community, and I saw the new convenience store owner probably once or twice a month. He was always very bright, and nothing bad ever happened to him.

I still knew Ed. I never stopped knowing anybody; I kept everything, like the books. I knew already that some people heal and some people don't, and I had my respect for both. I wondered if he had opened a new store somewhere else, or retired early, financially unwell—I wondered whether he had a decent place to live. I hoped he had a family that would take care of him.

Oil on canvas. What did artists have besides so much time? They had us, asking to see our own worlds anew, or past worlds alive. And what did they think of those they painted? Did they love them, or pity them, or forget them even as they stood there in the room, waiting in the light? I admired their colours but I saw everything already, and I had the time. I was awake. Smoking cigarettes in the night, sometimes for hours, I remembered the racks of smokes behind Ed when he sat in his store, reading the paper, before he was hurt. Looking up sometimes, then looking down.

BODIES

ALI'S FATHER WOKE HIM UP EARLY.

"I need your help getting bags from the car; I forgot them," he said.

Ali put on his track pants and hoodie and zipped it up close to his chin, then pulled the hood over his head. He was sleepy and annoyed but not showing it to his father—or trying not to. It took him a few tries to get his shoes on. His father was already dressed for work and wearing a parka, zipped up, holding the keys and waiting by the door.

It was bitterly cold outside. It bit through Ali's body and woke him up quickly. "What did you forget?" he asked his father, feeling that talking would keep him warm. He kicked up his step a little as well.

"The rice," his father said. "I bought a lot of bags."

"It's frozen now," Ali said.

"I can't let it sit there all day again."

"Okay." Ali didn't know how else to keep the conversation going.

They had a red Nissan that was older than most cars you see around and had rust along the bottom of the passenger side. It was far away, beside the park, because they didn't have a space in the building—his father found street parking each night. They approached the red car, and behind it they could see the park. There was a cold mist above the frozen, white-tipped grass—thick. A long, black object lay in the field, not too far from the road; it was just past dawn and the light was still very blue.

Ali's father popped the trunk and started handing several cold, sagging sacks of rice to him. The burlap sacks had handles at the top; they were heavy, and Ali took two in each hand. It was his father's favourite brand, but the supplier hadn't delivered last week; he had driven out to a store to get them. Ali's father closed the trunk with a few bags to himself, but they both paused and looked again into the park. In the mist, it was about the length of a person. Or a lot of crumpled clothes laid out in the shape of a person.

They started walking back to the building.

"Was that a man in the park?" Ali asked.

"I don't think so," his father said. "It's too cold for that."

/ / /

Ali found it difficult to fall back asleep. He was still painfully cold under the blanket, though he curled his legs up closer to his body. After a while, he could sense that it was close to the time he would be getting up anyway. He got out of bed and took a shower.

They lived in one of those older buildings that had small windows in the bathrooms. It seemed odd from the outside—all these tiny windows going up along the edge of the building where the bathrooms were—but in fact he loved it. Early in the morning, the bright blue air, or lazy and late in the summer, the golden light. It made him take long showers, longer than he needed. He left the lights off and used only the early daylight in the small bathroom.

He went to the kitchen where his mother was making tea for herself. He didn't know what to say to her about getting the rice and seeing something in the park. He stood next to her and started warming up some bread while she was stirring her tea and putting away things in the cupboard. She sat at the table and Ali followed her.

It was quiet for a few moments—his mother was a serious woman with few but often heavy words—and then Ali cleared his throat and said, "I think there was a body, a man, lying in the park this morning."

She looked at him sharply. "In the park? How do you know?"

"I was helping dad get bags from the car. He woke me up. Maybe an hour ago."

She blinked a few times, trying to put it together. Then her eyes and mouth became hard and angry, which Ali did not understand. She had many emotions, although she was quiet, but she was not usually quick to anger.

"Don't walk past there to school," she said briskly. "He's probably just sleeping it off."

Then she drank from her tea.

Ali knew it was too cold to be sleeping.

"It's drugs, you know," she said, with anger in her voice. She was almost accusing him. "Drugs."

/ / /

Apparently no one called the police. And she was right; it probably was alcohol or drugs. It looked like an overdose.

Ali walked up to the body on his way to school, with both Kal and Pete from the building, and of course Pete was very eager about it, as Ali knew he would be. The grass was crisp and made a sharp sound as the three of them walked. It wasn't as bitter cold as it had been earlier that morning, and the mist had risen. They all stopped a few feet away from the body, looking down. Pete swore under his breath—a dead body, flat out.

Pete took photos, including up close to the man's face, which was a cold grey colour. The skin around the eyes was darker, bluer. Ali did not get close and his heart was beating quickly. Ali stood, mostly facing Kal, who was not looking at the body either. But from where he stood, and what he saw of the face, the eyes seemed to be slightly open. Ali thought he could see white between the eyelashes. "Let's go," Pete said, and the three of them turned and walked away.

Pete was on his phone for the rest of the walk to school—Ali guessed most of the school would know before anyone even thought to call the police. And he was right.

A lot of kids talked about it that day, including several who actually came up to him and said, "You saw it first?" Ali said that he had, and explained being woken up by his father just after dawn to get bags of rice from the car, which later he thought was an unnecessary detail. Still, being asked about something a couple times was a new experience for him. By the third time answering, he was more comfortable and talked longer.

It wore off late in the afternoon. The photos had been shared, people had made jokes, and the body had been removed from the park by the police. People were talking about it less. Even as it faded, it left a vague feeling with Ali—like he was older, and also restless, as if he were waiting to be alone. He wanted to think about it by himself. He could still see the park under the heavy white fog in the blue light, and the black object lying in the grass.

/ / /

The truth was—which he told no one at school—he knew the guy. He had seen him before, many times. It was the guy with the dreadlocks.

The guy with the dreadlocks hung around the strip mall east of their building, out of the way of school, but not too far. The guy was very thin and tall, light skinned, with teardrop tattoos under each eye. His dreads weren't very long; they brushed the tops of his shoulders and danced around his head when he talked or gestured. He often wore baggy pants and thick skater shoes. He sometimes asked people for spare change, depending on the person, what kind of car they were getting out of, and whether he could see in their eyes that they were afraid of him or pitied him. But many people visiting the strip mall were regulars, and he chatted with them. He also had tattoos covering both arms and occasionally seemed drunk or high or both. The guy with the dreadlocks would recognize Ali, too. At first it was just a nod; then later he would say, *hey man*.

For a long time, Ali was scared of the guy with dreadlocks, from when he was nine or ten years old and first going to the corner store by himself. As a boy he had been fascinated by the dreads but felt fearful of the tattoos on the man's face and arms. But later, as the man started acknowledging him with *hey man* and it was clear he would not say anything else to him, Ali felt more comfortable. And a few times, the man looked messed up, sitting outside the corner store and slumping over—and Ali understood that he was sick, sad or troubled. Why else would he drink or take stuff to do that to himself? When he pitied him, the fear more or less went away. And then a year ago, he heard an older man in the convenience store talk about the guy with dreadlocks—a foster kid and then homeless for a while. No family. Now he was in a shelter, but he couldn't drink there.

He was still thinking about it at dinner, but not planning on saying anything. But his little sister did.

"I heard they found a body in the park today," Naya said. "They said at school."

Ali's mother said quickly, as if she was expecting it, "I heard too." She was quiet for a few moments and then started to look angry again. "These people do drugs in the parks, and they pass out—"

Ali's father made a murmur, short of actual words—a sound that said *don't*—to his wife.

"—overdosing or whatever they call it," she said. She looked at her husband, and still had anger, hurt in her eyes. "And then children walk by and see it," she said.

"Well, he's dead," Ali said. "So it's over."

There was an abrupt silence. He hoped this would end the conversation. He was thinking the eyes might have been slightly open all night, the mist obscuring the black sky and its tiny stars, and he remembered the hard white-blue lips—he wanted to be alone with his thoughts. His sister would not respond to what he had said, but he did not know about his mother.

It was quiet for a few minutes as they ate together. His father looked pensive and calm, chewing his food with a loose jaw, relaxed. His mother was eating less, but briskly. She wanted to say more to her children, help them understand.

"They do it for fun; they get addicted," she said. "You can't hang out with people like that. You stay away from that. You see your friends doing that, you get away—you understand?"

Naya was nodding and looking at her plate.

Ali looked at his mother. He knew so much about her, things she didn't realize he knew. He knew, for instance, how she had spent the last months with their dying dog—a creature she had no use for during its entire life, and in fact appeared to occasionally despise, particularly after any mess. She hated cleaning up after it, hated the fur. And it was often noisy. But the dog was for the children, and so it was cared for and stayed alive for a long time—until it was dying, and one day refused to eat. Normally they would put the bowl on the floor and the dog would eat. But now they would put the bowl down and the dog would not get up—just looked at the bowl and looked away. It seemed the dog was giving up. But his mother, one night, sat down in frustration on the floor after she had scraped out the old food and put out fresh food—the third time in a row—and still the dog had not approached. So she sat down on the floor. Frustrated, and sad to see the dog was dying. Sad to know the children would cry. But when she was on the floor next to the bowl, the dog got up and walked over, and standing next to her, he slowly started to eat. And although it took him a long time, he finished the meal.

And so, for months after that, while the dog was dying but now deciding to try not to, she would put the bowl down and sit quietly on the ground next to it. And Ali remembered the mornings walking into the kitchen and his mother sitting on the floor. And she was very quiet and still. She sat on the floor with her legs out comfortably, as sometimes it would be fifteen minutes or more. It was such a jarring sight for him. Not only her on the kitchen floor, which otherwise would have been inconceivable, but how still she was—the years of disliking the dog, and now this. The dog would finish the meal, slowly, and then she would stand up and take the bowl to the sink. Her seriousness about everything. Her stubborn heart.

Ali took another shower before bed, which usually he did not do.

The bathroom was cold and he pulled off his clothes quickly. He stood facing the stream and felt the hot water lighting up the surface of his skin—eyes closed, he imagined himself glowing gold with heat. Warm bodies going cold; his cold body going warm. His memory was vivid, crisp—the wet grass, the fog, the body—everything cut with dark blue lines.

Ali didn't understand why his mother was so angry about the body, and about drugs. Why she hated them. Ali knew the guy with the dreadlocks and the other guys in the neighbourhood who got messed up—they were all dying before the drugs ever came. They were often shit poor and always forgotten, drunk parents, no parents, sisters that ran away, disappeared—abandoned, abused, ignored. Drugs weren't for fun; they were for the turning over of another day, for a moment of not being there. At last. Their whole lives—they were dying and no one would sit with them.

Ali expected his mother would know that, but she didn't. And he did not know how to tell her.

STUPID

K WAS YOUNG FOR A VERY LONG TIME. She coloured her hair playfully and tried to stay curious and loose about life; it seemed many people were going in the opposite direction as they got older, especially into their forties and fifties. Becoming rigid, starting to calcify. And then others just lost their minds. Had a few kids, disappeared in the work. They didn't go crazy, necessarily; their minds just wandered away and never came back—they lost them. And the remaining years were spent in front of a television, eating noodles.

It was important to be a little contrived, K thought. To show a little effort. And she dressed a little bit that way and talked in a manner that was noticed in public. She was lively, undisciplined. Other people said she was colourful and eccentric, and she did not take offence, though secretly she did not want to be described this way—secretly she wanted to be elegant. But brightly lit.

She had worked for a newspaper when newspapers were still around. You know those pages that used to list the movie showtimes? She had designed those pages in a program, every night. She did it full time for almost eighteen years. She couldn't quite remember what she wanted to be when she was a kid, but she was pretty sure it didn't start with *You know those pages that used to show the movie times?* She also helped with sports scores at night. You didn't need an education for the job—she had applied to an opening for data entry. She imagined that if someone had to go to school and they ended up doing what she was doing, they would be pretty disappointed with their life.

But it was a union job and paid briskly. And so eighteen years went by. They weren't unhappy years but there was a blankness to them, as if daytime passed without a change of colour, without maturation. Like leaving a theatre when it's still light outside. It was a long stretch, and she did not have all of her happiness available; it eluded her in ways she did not understand. She worked there with a few colleagues who pleased her, but then newspapers started disappearing, and when her paper started talking about layoffs and offering buyouts, she took the money. They signed a card for her and bought her a strawberry cake. She had savings and her severance pay, although not much of an idea what she wanted to do next. She was unmoored, gently adrift.

/ / /

K only ever loved one man. And it wasn't the man she was married to for eight years during her time at the newspaper—her husband had been a good friend to her; they were still friends even years later. But when she left the paper, she was making a bigger break. She had coloured the edges of her hair blue and started wearing big earrings, even though she was no longer young.

R was muscular and masculine, reserved and reliable. A Marlboro man. There was something intelligent and watchful about his distance from everyone. But he was also a man rooted in vice, preferring almost nothing else in the world to sitting alone and drinking—attending to everything else with great, calm patience but clearly not alive in it. His father before him drank, as did the father before his father. The men of his family were too chest-tight for this world; one uncle became a devout athlete, running off whatever it was he needed to run off, but the rest drank. Still she loved that man. And he was more or less around; he liked to drink at home. Some men just seemed hard to find in the evenings, skittering off into the shadows.

He was serious when he first met her. He worked in building maintenance and rescued her from a stairwell where she had been trapped, forgetting her pass card, not wanting to walk down to the bottom. She had heard footsteps and called out, her voice soaring above and below, until the steps came closer. She laughed and thought the entire thing was funny, her face showing a bright interest in him; he was polite but stared at her, almost coldly. He was brusque with her the next couple of times they saw each other, briefly, in passing. But it all fell apart at a bar one night, the one nearest to the office. They recognized each other immediately. He finished a glass of scotch quickly and became flippant with her. She scoffed. Drunk, he was gripped with a desire to flip her over and pin her on the ground and hold her there as long as he could, forever. He felt it all over his body. She could read something in his face—he was somehow tied up in her. She was impressed by him, physically, and his broad, old-world features. So okay, she said, then call me.

They drank together and ate dinner and watched movies and fell asleep. It became clear after some time that he was not making love to her. She did not speak of it or clamour for him at night as they slept in the same bed. She sensed something in him waiting. Perhaps it was apprehension, something he did not show at any other time of the day, in any other situation. She wondered about that. But more time passed, and she grew restless, turning away from him and, during the day, letting her hand fall from his. It had some apparent effect on him and one night he roughly clutched at her, pinned her and held her, was almost panicked as he pulled covers back and held her body, all over. And the next day, he was relieved—cracking a smile at her when her back was turned, when he thought she did not see him. But she caught it in the kitchen window glass. And so, with him, it became a panicked thing. He would not make love to her until he was almost panicked by it, sickened with it, and with fear he was losing her. She grew accustomed to it but wondered why it was always that way. Why he would wait until fear gripped him, for days and then weeks.

It wasn't always entirely clear why she loved him. She sat with that idea sometimes. He was drinking daily, at home, alone. Some nights she helped him into bed and put a glass of water beside him. They rarely went out together. They had no children; it was a secret she could keep from everyone because they were not social people. But the greys were collecting on her head, and she wondered if she could really keep it up for the next few decades until one of them died, and it struck her, suddenly, how sad it was to even perform that calculation. So, she would end it.

/ / /

She remembered the conversation they were having when she knew. He had folded his arms across his heavy chest and was avoiding looking at her. She had asked why he never wanted to do anything, go anywhere; she said it playfully, but it threw something dark across his eyes.

"I don't need to, K," he said.

"Don't need to what?" she asked. "Leave the house?"

"No, I don't need to leave the house." They were sitting at a small diner close to her apartment, where she had asked to go, drinking black coffee after he had stumbled on her living room rug and knocked a plant down. He was embarrassed by it, and she used that to get him to come to the diner. "I go to work, I come home—then I'm home."

She looked around the small restaurant without emotion. There were two older women having a plate of pie each. They had dressed well, wearing silk scarves and wool blazers. The man from the counter was walking by with coffee. It was an old-fashioned diner, which she liked, and not very popular.

"I like leaving the house sometimes," she said.

"I know," he said. "It's good for you." He held the small coffee cup in his hands, looking down into the black circle. "The world is good for you."

He seemed to emphasize the word *you*, but she didn't rise to it. She let it fall silent for a couple of minutes. She was making a decision about him. She had that calm feeling.

"You want to be alone?" she asked him.

"No," he said.

"Order some food," she said.

"I'm not hungry," he said.

They sat across from each other without saying anything more. He was always comfortable with that; she was not.

R was so self-contained—she thought, resentful—his bulk, his head, all made of dense black rock. Impenetrable. He would be the exact same no matter where he was; twenty years older or younger, he would still be sitting here in the exact same way—nothing outside made its way in. And yet, other times, he was so shy he could hardly look at her. Was he very near or very far away?

He leaned forward on the table, elbows down.

"The truth is," he said, "I don't understand so many people having to leave home so many nights, having to travel, having to drive—to bars, for air—having to leave. They have to leave and come back to feel good. I don't understand it."

This surprised her. K never thought R would ever start a sentence with, "The truth is." He was never philosophical about himself, or life, never attributing any small thing to a greater thing.

"When you have a home, that's it," he said, opening his hands. "You don't need to leave, to come back, to make it home."

"So, am I the home?"

His head tilted slightly to the side.

"Mm." The sound was small and tight. He was looking down into his hands.

She looked at him, calmly, trying to see everything and see it plainly. But R had an intelligent, aware body. It knew when to expand and assert, and when to surrender, an older intelligence than her own sensitive, watching one. She could challenge him with words, but somehow he could change her mood, suppress the room, colour the air with his body's gentlest inflections. She could not control how much control he had over her and everything else—when he was vulnerable, it muted her.

She looked around the diner again, considering it—she had escaped her own safe, half-coloured life, and now she would be pulled into his. Did that bother her? Why, or why not. And wasn't he truly himself while drinking, alone? What, exactly, was home.

The old women in the diner were getting up to leave, pulling on gloves. One of them looked up and smiled. For a moment K felt a slim thread of understanding pass between them.

/ / /

Home. That smell in the summer when the first evening got cool—that very first evening—and you knew that summer was ending. How it felt in your lungs at dusk. It was weeks or months away but the season, in its subtlest shades, was turning. You were suddenly reminded of it in a way that held you in the stomach—tightly—and the chest. Lungs clutching at sharp air. Air cool as water.

So you went home, and it got dark outside, and you put on the television and made something to eat. And you felt suddenly quite calm with the meal ahead and tucked in with the TV. It didn't matter about the evening being cool, and summer ending. It smelled warm and still, and indescribable to anyone else. It was a world belonging to children, K thought. Sleepy-limbed, heavy-eyed. Safe and tired and home.

/ / /

"You always have to wait for some kind of tragedy to appreciate things like this," Elizabeth said.

She was standing in front of a big bay window with a tree outside. It was late spring. "Crisp maple leaves against a blue sky, gently waving in the wind," she said, gesturing with a thin hand. "Guaranteed if we weren't here for a funeral, I wouldn't be looking at it." She waited to find more words. "It's almost beautiful."

Simon was sitting in an armchair, facing her at the window. "This is a pretty town," he said. He noticed the tree was actually an oak.

"Technically a suburb," Elizabeth said, still looking out the window. She was K's sister. "No density, but some parts look like a town as you're driving through it. Doesn't really have a central area, except for a mall."

Elizabeth was a grant writer and lived in the city. A smart woman, educated, with good instincts. After she recovered from the shock and the tears, Elizabeth turned brittle, thinking coldly of what had happened. R had called the ambulance, saying it was an accident. It wasn't clear why he was over at K's place, but they were arguing, he had been drinking, it was an accident. She had fallen and hit her head; she didn't have any other bruises on her. The police weren't able to determine whether R pushed her or not because only three or four days later he drank himself to death—his body a few miles from the bar, in the direction of home. Literally in a ditch.

Elizabeth didn't know much about R. He didn't get out much, it seemed. And K had always visited her without him. He was old-fashioned—did not speak very often, was not online at all, maybe guarded, maybe uncomfortable around other people. He was admittedly handsome. But he was almost shy about it, as if he carried it self-consciously.

And he drank. Now her sister was dead, his body had been found in a ditch, and the story was over.

"When a woman is killed, it's often someone she knows—often it's the ex," Elizabeth said. "Violence against women is a huge issue in this country." She was still facing the window. "In all countries."

Simon had his fingers laced together, legs crossed; he was looking into the wool fabric of his pants spanning out in front of him. He was more than a decade younger than Elizabeth, tall like she was, and reed thin. He had been alone for a long time before meeting her, and they had married quickly, without a show.

"I wish she had told me she needed help," Elizabeth said. "Getting out."

"Maybe she didn't know she needed help," Simon said.

"That's true."

People die for all kinds of reasons, Elizabeth thought. People fall off things, fall down stairs, eat or drink themselves to death, get smashed in cars. Women get in fights with men; there are accidents. That was the shit truth. What had happened was not so unusual; it just felt early. Elizabeth didn't think she would have to attend anyone's funeral for at least another ten years. She did not think she would be here, now, for K.

They were going to be in town for three days.

Elizabeth had wheat-coloured hair; it had been more of a soft brown when she was young, but it had greyed early and steadily, and she did not care to dye it. K had been shorter and darker. K was all their mother, Elizabeth was all their father, with very little overlap.

Elizabeth was born first, garrulous and bold, relishing attention and responsibilities, and with that role assumed above her, K grew up in a hazier focus, a dreamy girl freed to roam. But they had had a good relationship. They didn't always understand each other but each was patient, both learning to be generous and affectionate as sisters, better at it in their thirties and later. Elizabeth did not hear much about female friends, and she wondered if she had been one of the closest people to K, even though they were not in touch so often.

She left the window and sat on a sofa. Simon looked over at her and then back to the window where she had been standing.

"She loved him," Elizabeth said. "She really did. She told me that. But she was leaving him." She paused and looked around the room. "She was kind of an eccentric, I guess you could say. She had interesting hobbies. She left that newspaper job and then lived off the severance for a bit. Then a few office jobs, then the bookstore job, living cheap. She would make these bracelets and sell them." Elizabeth made a circle with her fingers and thumb—an "O" shape—holding it up to show Simon. "They were rigid bracelets, like a bangle, but still made with beads."

"You have the gold one," Simon said.

"That's right," Elizabeth said. "I wore it once." She was leaning back into the soft sofa, sinking in. Her dress was dark purple, almost black. Her legs were bare, even though it was cool outside, and she wore black suede shoes.

"She used to dye her hair oddly—usually just the ends. Bleaching and then adding bright colours on top. Green, blue, red, orange. I said, you'll destroy your hair. She said, it's just hair. Have some fun."

"She was colourful," Simon said.

"That's true."

Elizabeth exhaled, arms lying on either side of her on the sofa. Then she folded them across her chest and cocked her head, considering something. Then she unfolded them again.

She looked at Simon and thought of R—the two men could not have been further apart, even with how little she knew about the other man. She and her sister had made different decisions. And that small, blinking disappointment had sat in the background for years: the dreamy and unheeding younger sister following her own unclear path when Elizabeth had carved a straight one. Elizabeth had wanted K to follow. Elizabeth had wanted K to be safe. She took a fuller breath and exhaled it slowly. And now she was here.

She admitted to herself that she had expected things to happen—she'd had misgivings. She thought she might have to loan her sister money someday; she might even need to offer a place to live, maybe when they were very old. K could never buy a place. A trailer, maybe. She might have ended up in one, but down south or on the West Coast, where it was warmer and milder. Making crafts and selling small things like that. Living cheap. She was eccentric and could have been happy but Elizabeth knew the truth of the situation—K could have done and been so much more, and instead chose this. Never had kids, no career either; she rejected both. She never did the work everyone else was doing. A child her whole life, a place she did not want to leave.

Elizabeth made order of it in her mind. Their paths were clear, and once she understood it, she felt cold about it, resigned; she turned away from grief. A tragedy was only when it didn't make sense.

She felt calmer, with order restored.

"If he hadn't killed her—if it had just never happened at all—she probably would have said she still loved him best," Elizabeth said. "The love of her life. If he hadn't killed her, she would have felt that."

Simon did not know what to say. He did not know K very well, and had never met R.

Elizabeth's mouth turned down, considering. "I think she was stupid like that."

THE APARTMENT

SHE SEEMED TO DO ALMOST EVERYTHING NAKED. Baking, cleaning, reading a magazine, exercising—it was a kind of bouncing, as we called it. She wore shoes then, with socks, and she pulled them up.

She lived in an apartment across the street, a few floors lower than us. We were renting a two-bedroom condo from one of those absent landlords who snap up a bunch of units and rent them out to pairs of young people trying to stay in the city, landlords you never hear from until they raise rent. But it was a nice building, and an absent landlord—always in Beijing or Montana or somewhere in Europe—was better than a crazy landlord who checked the place once a month, or who left strange messages for you, or Adam, more specifically. That had actually happened to him twice. One was an older woman; one was an older man.

She was already there when we first moved in but it took a while to notice her. She wasn't that easy to see, across the street and a few floors down—a flesh-coloured mass at first, until Adam dug through the storage unit and his camping gear to find his binoculars, and then a quiet evening descended as we stood at the window, passing the binoculars back and forth. We didn't talk for a while. But it had to be asked aloud. Exhibitionist? Nudist? Weirdo? But she looked too normal. Nymphomaniac? There wasn't evidence of that either. Narcissist?

Adam was single, so was I. That was the basis of being roommates. We met on a softball team, and he was new to the city, having taken a big corporate job. I had been here all my life, but most people I had known had left the city after a handful of disappointments, usually work-related. Or a friend would find a serious girlfriend and she would want to leave, so they would both go—women were always wanting to leave. They would find a guy and then they would leave. At some point, it seemed that most of the people that stayed were single, or gay, or the power couples—affluent and tattooed and cool—or the loner types that continued through their thirties in the basement apartments hidden throughout the city, not trying to change anything. Happy, I guess. Mostly men, playing video games, a more rewarding kind of reality.

But Adam was trying, really trying, as some guys do. He was working out and on all the apps. He had hair removal done on his back. And he was doing well at work, he said. If he smelled a promotion, even in another department, he chased it down and cornered it like prey—he had the right attitude to do well in the city. Whenever he got good news about work, he always said, "It's my biannual promotion." Some things about him you just couldn't make up. He once dated a stylish, artsy girl and got her to take him shopping; together they went to the best shops and he got all the fitted shirts and pants, and they even did the quirky shops, so he got some cultured t-shirts and one vintage coat with a high collar and extra buttons. He looked great; he filled his wardrobe. Then he dropped her. He said they hadn't even had sex—he didn't want to use her for that. Adam had goals; he was cruel, but in a non-personal way. It was hard to be offended or point out what was wrong, exactly—it was never about you.

He was once with an older woman and she grew obsessed with him, coming by our place at strange hours and sitting in the hallway. Later he was with another older woman, but she dropped him pretty quickly—he was angry for months. But he dated through that too.

I had met Adam's parents twice. They stepped into the apartment as they were picking him up for dinner. They were both short, and his dad had a gentle squint when his mom spoke, which was often and eager. It was hard to see Adam in them; it seemed he had decided to go a different way with his life.

We made an odd pair. We actually didn't go out much together; I wasn't exactly part of the official narrative. But he would come home and I would be there—half-waiting for him, most nights. How was work; where did you go after. Sometimes I would be standing at the window with the binoculars, but I would quickly leave when I heard the fumbling at the door. When Adam looked out the window, it was in an amused, leisurely way, unashamed and curious, sometimes thoughtful. Then he'd forget all about it and go back to his day.

She'd have friends over and she would wear clothes for them; perhaps that was to be expected. But they would leave, and she would slip out of everything and maybe put on a robe—a grey one, hanging open—and then naked for the rest of the night. She must've had the thermostat up to thirty. I never saw a woman without blankets in the evening. We could not figure out why she did it. Why, why—it was like a nightmarish apparition that visited us during the day—*why*. Nothing seemed to make sense.

Meanwhile, in the building, men were starting to make elevator trips with telescopes. I even saw powerful filming equipment with a long, professional lens, which I told Adam about—it all came new, in boxes. We saw at least three or four of them—one guy had a wedding band, seemed old enough to be a father. Adam was disgusted with that. But apparently that was the way the world worked. Lots of things weren't pleasant but if you saw enough people doing it, you learned to ignore it.

One day, Adam came home out of breath, animated, tripping over his words. "The naked—the woman in the window—"

I was cooking in the kitchen, pasta—making extra in case he came home for dinner and was hungry—and I stopped everything and met him in the doorway. "What, what?"

"In the store—I went to the store. I saw her at the store. I recognized her face," Adam said.

"What happened?" I asked.

"I got her number."

He got her number.

It fell flat with me. At this point I was getting bored of the whole thing. I was tiring of the voyeurism and frustration, a repetition of other areas in my life. I had given up on a lot in the past couple weeks, something Adam hadn't noticed. My aunt had died in a violent way—a man she was breaking up with—and that started my mom drinking again, which hadn't happened in decades, and something was going downhill back home. I was getting drunk emails, alternating between how much she loved me as a son to more detailed complaints about old friends or family. The guy was arrested in another city and brought back and there was going to be a trial next year.

"I got her number," he said.

His face was uncharacteristically eager.

"Well, why don't you text her then?" I said, and went back into the kitchen.

/ / /

I once saw him throw a chair across the room, dead sober. He got so mad that time the Leafs were destroyed by Boston—he got that hard stare, and you couldn't even talk to him.

He actually didn't drink that much, but I was starting to drink a bit more. At first I would pour a glass of wine while making dinner—eventually it would be an hour before dinner, and then right when I got home from work.

Adam called the naked woman and seemed to implement some kind of strategy, some game. He didn't take her out right away; he talked to her every day and stretched it out for days, a week, more. I had stopped going to the window, for the most part. But if he wasn't around, I looked quickly. Still naked.

/ / /

I didn't know what to make of her body. To be honest I wasn't sure she was that fit. Once the shock of the nudity wore off, it was maybe just above average. I had gone to the gym weekly for about a year, not too long ago, and I saw a lot of really toned women's bodies, sometimes even wiry, very fit. But the naked woman, I didn't know. In a couple months, it didn't seem as much.

She dressed well, though, for work and when guests were coming over. I thought she dressed elegantly, but prettily, and not out of reach. But then she would be cleaning, nude, squatting under furniture, and I thought that maybe the whole thing was growing tiresome. I was down in the basement of our building, dumping our recycling box, and I saw scrawled on the wall near the stairwell doors, *5th floor*—apparently it was not so tiresome yet to other men.

She had a routine, something I picked up on fairly quickly and Adam never seemed to notice, or at least he never said so. I had routines too—I saw them in others. She came home and put her bag on the brown chair. Nothing else seemed to go on that brown chair except her slouchy bag. No one ever sat in it. She poured a glass of water right away and let it sit on the counter as she tended to a few minor things—checking her phone again, or putting something she had bought in the fridge, or taking her shoes from where she kicked them off back to their proper place, at the bottom of the closet by the door. It was a small apartment; she was conscientious about putting her things away. And then she would leave the phone somewhere—kitchen counter, or still in her bag—and sit on the sofa, unselfconsciously, her legs somewhat splayed, and she would look out the window.

I don't know what she saw from that window, but sometimes, walking along the street, I would glance up to see from her view. It was of another building, not ours, a thicker and older structure from the '80s or '90s, with beige cement and pale green windows—unattractive, not old enough to seem interesting either. It couldn't have held her eye. But there was a park beside it, a simple one with circles of cultivated flower beds situated throughout the small green rectangle and almost half a dozen wooden benches. The bench-to-tree ratio seemed a lot higher than other parkettes I'd known downtown. Maybe she would look down at the people on the benches. Beyond the park, there were old stone row houses, conspicuously distinct from each other—new homeowners had upgraded their home fronts with matte painted brick and sharp window dressings, and inherited owners had covered the glass with foil and had air-conditioner boxes hanging out. One of countless patchy stretches in the city—rich, rich, rich, poor, poor, rich, poor, rich, rich.

And then she would go back to the kitchen and drink the glass of water. It happened this way, or something very close to it, every day.

/ / /

Adam was dating her and examining it very closely with me. It was rare that he would become suddenly talkative and animated, so I didn't mind. In fact I came to enjoy it. Adam was an okay guy—or there was something moral about him sometimes. But the rest of the time he was just so casually selfish in all things, like he never bothered to know anybody else. Like he was always okay alone and had stopped even thinking about it—this idea of other people.

He didn't think she was an exhibitionist. He had researched the term and decided it didn't sound like anything about her. Nudist or weirdo or hippie? He was really favouring these possibilities, wondering if there was a modern version of hippies that she was embodying—but there were associations with those words. Negative or annoying. He couldn't imagine that he would date a weirdo or hippie. At this point it had only been two dates and they hadn't had sex yet. So nymphomaniac was out. But they kept in touch throughout the week.

Narcissist? He paused each time after saying it, considering it. He had googled this word as well. "But it just doesn't suit her. I don't know."

We were sitting out on the balcony and drinking. It was a warm night, and we were both in t-shirts. I liked that about us, both in the same white tees. I could see he was relaxed and in a thoughtful mood. She wasn't at home—she was out somewhere, and he didn't know where. They hadn't texted that day. Still the binoculars were sitting on the balcony with us.

/ / /

She had a friend I didn't like. The woman had large, dark curly hair that bounced around when she talked, which was almost constantly. I imagined her voice was very loud. Her body language was open and energetic, and she flopped around on the furniture while describing big dramatic things. Frankly I thought she was vulgar.

Around her friend, I saw her body language, in response, become more subdued. Watching the energy between the women expand and contract, I felt this friend was draining. And I did not like when she visited.

But Adam was pulling the curtains down now. I didn't ask but guessed they were sleeping together. He was in her condo, pulling the curtains down after dinner. I guess he knew about all the perverts in our building, and likely the surrounding buildings, that were watching with above-average interest.

Not a nymphomaniac, weirdo, or exhibitionist. I tried to see that maybe she was a narcissist, but that seemed almost obscene. She was quiet, evasive, and slightly too open when she was happy, which was fairly often.

I was standing there for some time, with a glass of wine on the table beside me. Adam had not been home in two days. She was on the sofa, unguarded, looking at him often but also looking shyly away. It occurred to me then—seeing her happy and shy—that she was fully innocent. It was so simple. I was laughing and shaking my head, then I fell quiet again and looked through the binoculars.

She was an innocent.

/ / /

Adam hadn't been home in almost a week. I was drinking more, lonely and bored. He hadn't shown up to the softball game either and didn't text me why. Her curtains were down a lot.

When I heard the keys in the door, I jumped up. I was a bit drunk—watching that show that everybody at work was obsessed with, about the drug dealers who kill off each other's families and rape the wives, keeping their severed fingers in jars—and I stumbled as I hurried to get off the sofa. I knocked over my glass of wine. Adam was coming in as I was trying to save the glass in a sloppy commotion, half falling down—I could sense his face take it in and then perform an act of emotion I hadn't seen before. It seemed to be almost pity.

"Hey," I said, being casual, with some effort.

"Hi," he said. There was a pause. "I think that rug is a goner, though."

He was talking about the pale beige, patterned rug I had bought as a housewarming thing when we first moved in together. There was half a glass of red wine spilled across it. We were both looking at it, but with different emotions. I was patting at it with tissues from the box on the coffee table, very careful, a drunk's concentration.

And I started feeling angry all of a sudden.

A black emotion uncoiled inside me—he meets this girl and then disappears, coming home infrequently and not letting me know; now he comes back and looks at me with pity over a stupid rug.

"Fuck it," I said, standing up. "It's just a fucking rug."

I balled up the red tissues and went into the kitchen.

My tone said enough. Adam went into his room and was gone for half an hour. At first I came back and tried to clean the rug, hoping Adam would come out and see that I was working on it, but I got bored and returned to the kitchen for another glass, then went and sat by the window. She was in her apartment, dressed, lights on, curtains up, pacing around the space, collecting things and tidying up. She seemed to be brisk, in preparation, not wandering idly through it—I wondered if she was expecting him back tonight.

I was holding the binoculars when Adam came out and startled me, looking startled himself.

"You still look?" he said, genuinely surprised. He did not seem angry.

"Yeah, I still look," I said. "I guess you haven't even told her." I was still angry. "Maybe she would put some clothes on then."

There was a short silence. I waited, but nothing.

I followed up with a series of vulgar statements about her, including insults about her body, feeling a pathetic rage that somehow could not escape from me, not even with the words.

There was no pity in his face now—it went blank, impersonal. No anger either. There was a total and final detachment now. He was holding a gym bag, heavily filled.

I felt desperate, suddenly panicked, seeing that remoteness in his face, and that big bag. Held the anger around me, like armour. And I was drunk. "Get the fuck out of here," I said.

/ / /

After that, things started disappearing from the apartment.

He was doing it while I was at work, dropping by and picking up his stuff in trips. Her curtains were always down now.

He kept paying rent for three more months, until the lease expired. He had texted me earlier with notice—he wasn't coming back. I already knew that. His stuff was gone, and so was he.

I didn't respond. Things were already going to shit, so maybe none of it mattered. My mom was drinking too much, and so was I, so maybe none of it meant anything.

My aunt's ex-boyfriend was acquitted. And he just took off, left the town where they had lived about two hours up north. My mom was just basically ruined after that. I visited for a few days but she refused to talk about it, and I wandered around my childhood home, unsure what to do. Then I came back to the city to work—left my dad to take care of it. But she stopped emailing, and I'm not sure what she did for a length of time.

The woman moved out. Maybe Adam was with her; I didn't know—she wasn't on social media, and Adam never posted anything about girlfriends. The new people were a young couple with a toddler. I watched it learning to walk around one afternoon, feeling like it was very wholesome and meaningful in a way that actually mattered, big picture. But I was spending more time drinking in front of the television instead of looking out the window, and the binoculars ended up in the closet shortly after.

Financially, living alone was not easy. But I got a roommate in February and it was less stressful. His name was Jared and he was very quiet, almost silent, but not in a shy way—it was almost dark, obstinate. I thought maybe he didn't like people much. I didn't feel comfortable around him, but it was great because he kept to his room, so I still had the living room. Everybody at work was still following the drug dealer show, and they were killing off everybody now and raping the daughters; the series seemed to be ending very dramatically. Apparently it was the most watched show of all time. I watched it alone in the living room while Jared stayed in his room.

I did see her again, though.

I had half-forgotten her, and then suddenly there she was, in the convenience store buying soda. I was coming home from work and stopping to get water. She must have lived somewhere nearby—she was in house slippers—and I had never stopped in that store before. It seemed like something should happen.

I didn't recognize her at first with clothes on, standing in front of me, fully animated after a quick chat with the cashier, as if she were fully real—something that never seemed possible to me. She was walking past me and I said,

"Adam? You know Adam?" I didn't have anything planned.

"Yes," she said, stopping.

I was unprepared. She was looking at me.

"I know you. I used to live with Adam," I said. "When he met you."

Her face changed now, recalling something that she had heard about me, Adam's roommate. Up close, she was taller than I had thought. I felt electrified by her presence, standing in front me, simple and drop-shouldered, with a face bright and open. Eyes very large and kind. She did not seem shy at all. I wondered where that came from, that impression from a distance. I felt almost overwhelmed by her.

Her hair was past her shoulders and loose, tangled lightly, as if it moved around too much. It was coloured like dark sand. Her arms were bare. The intimacy of her, standing in front of me, was catching me by the throat.

"Right, Adam's roommate." She seemed less certain now. "How are you?" And I saw it again—her eyes seemed to turn down in the outside corners. It seemed like pity.

I remembered Adam's pity that night. It became clear that he did not care for me and never had, that he was seeing for the first time that I had cared all along. It was that impersonal pity, something you might give out to a stranger on the street who is suffering. No familiarity, no warmth—*we don't know each other*. He never once asked about my aunt, although I had told him about it. And I knew that all along, but denied it. I don't know what he told her about his roommate, but it seemed that she pitied me. Her large eyes were sympathetic.

Again, a dark emotion twisted in me, ugly. I grew angry. I didn't know why—I never knew why—people pitied me.

So I told her. I told her about the binoculars and the guys in the building and Adam's pursuit and game. I told her about how she put her bag down in the same brown chair and poured a glass of water when she got home from work. I said I thought she looked outside her window at the small park below. "You were his biannual promotion," I said.

You have no right to be innocent—this is the real world.

She was upset and left the store. I was upset as well and I walked out onto the street, looking both ways to see if I could see her walking away—why, I didn't know—but I didn't see her. I guessed they were still together. I also guessed Adam hadn't told her. About the binoculars and the guys buying telescopes, about us, discussing her, about all of us guys, everywhere.

And when I saw Adam again, it was many years later—as much as eight or nine. He was still fit; his face was leaner and he still dressed the same. When he recognized me, he smiled, shook my hand, and introduced his girlfriend—she was heavily tattooed on one arm, had a piercing in her cheek. Symbols that she was used to pain. But she was hot about it. Adam's face looked older, for sure. It was almost ten years, and I wondered what he'd think of me.

Out of nowhere, he asked about my mom.

I told him she had died.

He looked sad for a moment. "I'm sorry," he said.

DIVORCE

THEY HAD JUST MARRIED IN THE SUMMER, with family flying in from her hometown and two of his college friends driving ten hours to be groomsmen. It ended up being more expensive than they wanted, but it had acquired a certain momentum, and as the wedding got closer, they just hurried through the days until it was over, making costly decisions through exhaustion. Their friends had experienced it too—this was how it was for everyone. Finally it was done. They were relieved, and to calm down they ignored the line of credit for some time.

But within a few months, the landlord gave them sixty days. Her new husband was annoyed, but she wanted to see something optimistic in it—a fresh start, a new home. She knew they would throw out a lot of stuff during the move, and she wanted to buy new stuff—married stuff, acquired together, for their new place. All of a sudden, she wanted to paint. She was done with off-whites. She wanted a colour scheme and a mood in their home—and art. He agreed it sounded nice. The line of credit was already there—a hulking number they did not like to look at—and adding some more wasn't going to matter.

She found someone selling an oil painting online for only a hundred dollars. It was an original; you could see the brush strokes lifting off the canvas. It was a small sailboat in still water under a dusky sky cluttered with clouds. It was both vivid and thoughtful. Serene. She became excited and told her new husband and showed him the listing. But it's far away, he said—a train and two buses to get there. We can rent a car, she offered. He quickly added the cost of the rental to the price of the painting in his head but said nothing; he wanted her to be happy.

They got the car and reviewed the address, planned a route. She had five twenty-dollar bills in her wallet that she counted twice. She drove and chatted along the way; he watched the city slowly fade out into wide, quiet residential streets dotted with low brick bungalows. They hadn't rented a car in a while, and he had forgotten how slowly she drove.

"I just assumed it would go above the sofa, but I don't think we talked about it. That makes sense, right?" she said. She had never bought a painting before.

"Of course. It would look great there," he said. "We're always in that room."

"Exactly," she said. "This is an original painting. They didn't print it at a factory. It has to be the focal point."

It was a semi-detached house. She noticed immediately that one side was well kept and clean, and the other was a disaster, rundown.

"Which one is it?" he asked.

"It's 754," she said, pulling into the driveway, then leaving the turning light ticking. The rundown house. At the top of the driveway was a car encrusted with rust, with two flat tires visible from behind. She put the rental in park, still looking at the house.

"Ouch," he said.

She was recovering. "Glad you came with me," she said.

There was no doorbell so they opened the screen door and knocked and waited, standing on the stoop and looking around, wishing they were standing in front of the semi on the other side instead. They let the screen door close noisily. He felt this was a bad idea but did not want to say so; he imagined she was feeling the same. She was determined to get her painting and leave, but now was fearing there might be no painting at all.

A man opened the door. He did not look well; his thin beard was patchy, and his shirt appeared as if it had been worn for many days already. He squinted at them through the smudged glass. "Yeah?" he asked.

"I'm Leanne," she said. "I messaged about the painting."

She forgot to introduce her husband. "And I'm David," he said.

"The painting, yeah," the man said. "I'll get it. You have the money?"

"Yes, I brought a hundred dollars in cash," she said, relieved.

The man turned and left them standing on his stoop.

"Not too friendly," her husband said. She shushed him and took the bills from her wallet.

They were left standing there for a while. They looked at each other a few times and made expressions, but eventually she avoided her husband's eyes and looked around the lawn and the broken-down car in the drive. This was her thing, and he didn't want to say anything about it.

The man came back. She thought at first he didn't have the painting, and her heart quickly fell—she already feared the whole thing was a scam—but as he approached the door, he raised his arm and showed it in his hand. The painting was just slightly larger than a postcard, framed in delicate wood, small enough to hold in his palm.

They were speechless.

After a silence, the man said, "Here it is, then." He opened the door to hand it over and looked at the cash in her hand.

"It's so…small," she said. "It's…"

Silence fell again, and her husband said, "It's like a miniature painting?"

"Yeah," the man said. "It's like a miniature painting." He stared at them and waited to see how it was going to land. He knew the woman was upset.

Without looking at her husband, she said, "It's very delicate. It must have been hard to paint. Here you go." She gave him the bills, and he gave her the painting.

Neither side said thank you or goodbye. The couple left the door, and the man closed it.

They got in the car and pulled out of the driveway before they started speaking. He was waiting for her to talk first.

"It was just a photo up close. I guess there wasn't anything in the photo for scale. The posting didn't say the measurements. I hadn't even noticed. I just assumed."

The painting was in his lap and he held it up, examining it. "It's original. It must have been hard to paint. It's not so bad, Leeny." He used his nickname for her so that she would be less hurt. But it bothered her in that moment, as her disappointment had bruised her—pity made it worse.

They didn't talk for a while.

Eventually he held it up again. "So did he paint this?" he asked. "Or just sell it?"

"I don't even know," she said. "The posting didn't say—just 'oil painting for sale.' He didn't really look like a painter."

"Or," he offered, "he's one of those artists that are a bit weird. Reclusive, awkward."

"Yeah, maybe," she said. Aware of her husband's efforts, she still did not want them.

He looked at the painting for a while, then set it down in his lap and looked out the window.

The tiny painting could not hang above the sofa, or anywhere really—it was ridiculously small. She had it on the bookshelf for a while, but when she looked at it she always remembered the disappointment, the uncomfortable man, the rundown house. They bought a large print for the living room instead; it was abstract and modern and pleasant to look at. It was almost four hundred dollars and mounted in a polished metal frame the colour of champagne. Sometimes looking at it her mind went back to the tiny painting of the boat instead—it was the reason they had gone to a big store to buy this abstract print, renting a car again. Their line of credit had swelled.

Eventually she started putting glass baubles on the bookshelf and didn't think the small painting belonged anymore. She studied it, carefully, for the last time. It was a white sailboat. The sky was smoky with the colours of dusk—washed out blues, purples, and greys—and crowded with many clouds, heavy and solid in form, reflecting the colours of the sky. A few jets of gold lined the bottom of the clouds, the last impressions of a sun that had already disappeared from sight. Two or three wisps of black could have been birds in the distance. The ocean was completely still. It was painted like a mirror of the sky without a ripple across it. There were no people on the boat; it was empty. It was vaguely surreal. She knew it was beautiful.

But she resented the bitter disappointment and that the man had taken advantage of her and her husband, and she remembered her earlier excitement, her hopes for the new home, her optimism for their married life and its pleasant fulfillment of little wishes like this. An original painting centrepiece, a four-poster bed, copper-coloured pots. The little boat carried these lost little things.

She put the painting in a cardboard box in the closet.

/ / /

They stayed married roughly nine and a half years, falling just shy of a full decade, and had a daughter, eight, who was diagnosed with learning and emotional problems. They were always optimistic about her future when they discussed it, focusing on strengths and growth. But in a private place inside them they knew their daughter would struggle her whole life. They never once admitted to each other how deeply disappointed they were, never showed fear. So they grieved separately, and alone. The years accumulated on their marriage, and every frustration and disappointment amassed itself in their home. They fought about money. Weary, they became unkind.

She grew stout with disappointment, drinking too much wine and making cheesy pasta for dinner, over and over, blunted and soothed in front of the television with their daughter curled into her side. He grew distant, disapproving of how his wife coddled the girl but never uttering a word against it—there was too much pain there. He did not like to watch the same shows, so they got a separate television, which he watched in the other room. They no longer used nicknames for each other. When one of them found something dirty or forgotten in the house, they quickly blamed the other. Snapped with a cold white rage. Clothes on the ground, cheese glued to the pot—again. For the thousandth time. You never listen.

The divorce was ugly.

He had been injured seriously the year before—a car backing into him in a parking lot—and his recuperation took months. She cared for him during that time, attentive but unemotional. But he was shaken by the experience, felt his life was short, his body was aging—suddenly gripped by the realization of his slowly expiring life, he was unable to return to his marriage as the same man. Something else had broken. Without consulting her, he decided he wanted to be happy. He wanted a divorce.

She was stunned, and furious that he had done it first—secretly she had fantasized about divorcing him many times. But now? After she cared for him? After the injury? She did not admit anything to him and instead was victimized by his announcement. She started lashing out. He was calm and fair in the proceedings, but his magnanimity felt cruel to her—cold. As from a stranger. He was already fully detached from their life, and with such finality, while she was left with the emotional aftermath alone. So she told their friends unpleasant things about him; she called him while drunk, shouting into the phone. She told their daughter bad things, disfigured the truth. She started dieting and exercising aggressively, and they both hired lawyers, preparing for war.

But they were not alone during the divorce; so many of their friends were divorcing too. At this age, with children weaned and the trauma of toddlers behind them, people were leaving each other. It seemed almost a normal evolution in adulthood; this was how it was. She went out drinking with her friends, and they told horror stories about it. He talked about it with his friends, but not in the same way.

They battled over every single possession, neither side could stand the perception they were being bullied. Plates and towels and the scratchy boot mat. They still had the debt—an evolving entity in their marriage that they sometimes paid down and sometimes let climb, especially after having a baby—but they paid lawyers to carve out every cheap item in their home. She was furious—absolutely enraged—he even had the nerve to ask for the tall, rickety bookshelf that she had bought at the store, lugged back on the bus, and glued together herself. His lawyers told her lawyers that he had paid for it because he had reimbursed her later. It was four years ago; she didn't even remember that. She couldn't believe he would remember that.

"What's this about a painting?" the lawyer emailed. "He wants you to have it."

The lawyer was baffled because, so far, neither side wanted to let any single object go to the other person. She was upset by the note. She punched out her response—no, she wanted *him* to have it. His lawyers told him. He was incredulous—the painting had nothing to do with him. And he had made the decision in a moment of tenderness. She must be deranged to swat it away.

This did not belong with the lawyers. Defeated, she dropped the painting off at a thrift store, remembering again the disappointment, that unkempt man, her youth and hopefulness. She didn't even look at it one last time.

She was upset that he had wanted her to have it, seeing something malicious in it, almost jeering.

Both of them remarried quickly enough, sharing custody of their daughter. He married someone younger from work—which disgusted her—and she dated for a while before she found a patient, agreeable man with children of his own.

But the divorce had wounded both sides. They were bruised and tender. Each of them entered their second marriages timidly; they did not snap over chores or keep count of mistakes, they took deep breaths and said something funny instead, brushed it aside. They absorbed disappointments with a newfound steadiness, with sad-eyed humour, and humility, a calm ease with life and all its quiet losses.

Their friends remarried too. Second marriages seemed to stick. It was some years later when she saw the headline—"After artist's death, tiny paintings fetching tens of thousands"—and she did not even click on the article. Something flared inside her, an old wound. She paused long enough to see the photo, and it was another boat scene, but a little paler, a little plainer. She saw immediately that theirs had been more beautiful. She did not contact her ex-husband or tell anyone else about it; she didn't quite know what it meant.

FRIES SUPREME

HIS WIFE HAD THICK LEGS. I associated that trait with a man who takes no bullshit—and I was pretty right about that. Elliot took no bullshit. It was obvious enough that people had basically stopped trying to give it to him.

There were exceptions, though.

Of all professions, he was a teacher. He enjoyed the forthrightness of children. He was that one teacher in the school—usually there was only one or two—that was tough and remote and stood apart. Unbothered by everything. Kids naturally drifted toward him, and yet no one wanted to interact directly, except the very youngest, who were not self-conscious yet. And he seemed fine with that, standing around the yard at recess when it was his turn, often leaning on the fence, taking no specific interest in anything. He seemed sometimes as if he didn't belong—he could have been a mechanic, or perhaps with higher education, a pilot. Maybe he could have opened a business of some kind. There was something blank about Elliot, but commanding; he could have been important almost anywhere. He was big in almost every dimension: long limbed, big bodied, a large head with big features on it—forehead, eyes, nose, lips. There was a great empty calm around him. The children trusted him; the sensitive ones felt safe with his slow-moving figure in sight.

Elliot had lived in the city but left to work at our school in the suburbs. People were more relaxed out here, he said. There were big skies everywhere—no crowding of tall buildings at the edge of everything. Sunsets were bold; roads were wide and open. And he liked driving.

For school trips, teachers usually sat at the front in the bench seat behind the driver. But Elliot always moved around and often sat next to a kid who was solo on a bench. It was early May; we were driving north to a petting zoo. The children were eight and nine years old. Elliot sat next to a girl named Shivaun. I sat two rows ahead at the front, but I could hear him over the chatter of children.

"Hi, Shivaun," he said as he sat down.

"Hi," she said. She was smaller and quiet. Her hair was tied in two thick, loose braids that stood away from her head. She had plastic barrettes—one yellow, one purple. Under her denim coat, her shirt had a big horse face on it, and she was known to be shy.

"You don't mind if I sit here?" he asked.

"Sure," she said. "Yeah, you can."

She had the window seat and she tilted her torso toward it, looking out the window. Her small legs dangled. Beside her, Elliot was enormous.

The bus started up and they pulled out of the school lot, turning for the highway ramp about ten minutes away.

"Nice day," Elliot said.

"Mom said nineteen," Shivaun said, still looking out the window.

"Pardon?"

"Mom said it was going to be nineteen. She gave me my jean coat."

"That's a nice coat, Shivaun. I was going to say."

"Thanks." Smiling, she blushed.

We were on the highway. Suburban developments and cul-de-sacs gave way to farmland, stretches of green and yellow fields occasionally populated with a few cows. Small, dense forests seemed to have been cut into squares.

"How is your mom these days?" Elliot asked.

"She's good."

"Her health?"

"She says her back hurts sometimes."

"She injure herself?"

"Nah, it's work. She walks around a lot at work." Shivaun felt comfortable, open. "She has good shoes, but she says her back hurts. She went down to the basement to get our castle and all the pieces, but she moved the boxes around and hurt her back worse. We didn't go to the park either."

"I hurt my back in high school."

"How?" Shivaun turned on the bench to face him.

"Played football, running back. Running up the field and a guy gets me like this"—Elliot held his arm out, stiff—"cut me down like a tree."

Shivaun stared.

"Hurt my back. Still hurts sometimes. But I had to quit football and maybe that saved my head. If I had done it more, gone to college, I might have bashed my head up. Twenty years from now"—he pointed to his head—"all spaghetti upstairs."

She smiled, cautiously, at *spaghetti*. He grinned at her, sharing a joke. She smiled bigger and looked out the window again.

"But anyway," he said, languid, reminiscing. He looked out the window with her and contemplated the passing fields. Cows never seemed to move much, except the gentle swish of a tail—on the way home, they would still be standing there, just like that. "The back still hurts sometimes, and I'll always remember that hit," he said.

Shivaun was thinking. "I'm sorry he hurt you," she said quietly.

"What's that?"

"I'm sorry that man hurt you. At home we say sorry when someone gets hurt."

"That's a nice thing," Elliot said. "If your mom taught you that, it's a nice thing to do. He wasn't a man; he was just a boy like me. I never really thought about the kid. We were playing a game—plus he said sorry later. Not right away but later when he saw I was pretty hurt. Coach and teachers said it too."

"That's good," she said.

They sat quietly for some time.

"Do you like the zoo?" Shivaun asked.

"I like the zoo all right," Elliot said. "If the animals look happy walking around in there."

"I like seeing them."

"I do too."

The bus took an off-ramp and merged onto another, smaller highway. There were fewer farmhouses now, wider expanses of land. The children were noisy, and a loud chatter rose up when they passed horses and a field with goats.

"You been to this zoo?" Shivaun asked.

"Every year," Elliot said. "The family seems nice enough. Seem to take care of the animals pretty well."

"I never been."

"You can tell your mom about it tonight, what you see. They've got parrots too—great big birds with colours you don't see anywhere. Not even paint or markers."

"I seen pictures," Shivaun said.

"Pictures are nothing. Wait until your eyes are on it. Wait until the wings open."

Shivaun's eyes were wide, watching his face.

"Are they mean?"

"That's a good question," Elliot said, considering. "I would say that they are very smart. I would say that if they wanted to be mean, they could be. Sometimes smart things can be mean things, because they know how."

"Do they bite?"

"I think if you did something to bother the bird, he might bite you, yeah."

Shivaun was speechless.

"I mean, it's a good zoo. The birds sit over there in their birdhouse, and we can look but we don't touch the birds. We don't put our fingers in."

The bus took another turn and slowed its speed on a two-lane road. Shivaun was silent.

"I would never bother the bird," she said, quietly, after thinking. "I hope I don't bother it by accident, or if I do, the bird knows it's by accident."

"They're very smart and they would know it's by accident," Elliot said, smiling. They were approaching the zoo. "But we don't put our fingers in."

The bus unloaded; the kids milled around excitedly in the parking lot. Shivaun went to a small group of girls and stood near them. Elliot stood apart, stretching his arms across his chest.

We spent the morning looking at goats, deer, reptiles, and birds. Elliot walked along without saying anything or talking to anyone. He looked in at the animals and then walked on, quiet, on the periphery of the children. Shivaun stood at the front at the parrots' aviary, her eyes blinking rapidly in awe. At lunch the children went to the diner across from the zoo—a tiny place intended for school groups. One unsmiling woman worked there, and she made several hot, brown dishes in large trays. There was a laminated sign propped up on the counter—*If you can finish our FRIES SUPREME, it's free!!!*

Bo, a tall boy with bright yellow hair, had been crowding along the diner's counters as he watched the thin woman preparing the food. He pointed to the sign. "Mr. Brock should eat it!" he cried, waving his arms and attracting the other kids' attention. Bo struggled with impulse control, and his main social instinct was to rile up the other children to be more like him. "Hey everyone! Mr. Brock should! Mr. Brock, look!"

Children joined in the excitement. "Mr. Brock! Mr. Brock, look!"

Elliot walked up to the counter and studied the sign.

"Okay," he said.

The children screamed and cheered.

The diner woman looked at Elliot, her mouth set. She was a thin woman with a mean face, perhaps turned that way from serving screaming children, week after week, year after year.

"Yeah, I'll order this," he said to her.

The fries supreme was brought to the table, a pile of fat French fries—dark brown—that stood upright before him on the table, built like a small house. They were covered with sour cream, melted cheese, green onions, beef, fried beans, and tomatoes. Elliot looked up at the woman as she delivered them; both of their faces were inscrutable.

"Mis-ter Brock! Mis-ter Brock! Mis-ter Brock!"

It took Elliot almost an hour. He started slowly but quickly upped his speed, sensing his lack of progress after the first twenty minutes. The children stood around, but their attention wandered and they returned to their booths and benches to eat their own lunches. Some stood up and returned, visiting. Most of the chatter turned to the animals again. A thin coating of sweat shone on Elliot's face as he continued clearing the plate. The diner woman watched from the back.

"Wow, Mr. Brock," Shivaun said shyly. She had had fries with her lunch too but found they did not taste very good, and she did not finish them.

Elliot finished the fries supreme, and the woman took the plate, now for the first time appearing amused. She alone seemed to know the damage done. "It's free," she said.

The children cheered. He stood up and motioned that they should get back to the zoo. The children filed out in a state of animation. "The whole thing—he ate the whole thing."

Elliot sat out most of the afternoon. Without any of the children seeing, he managed to vomit behind the feed shed. As the children milled about between showcases and short, sit-down talks, he sat outside on a bench, looking off over the buildings, his face still sweating. A few kids would wander over, asking how he was. Invariably he said, "Actually, I'm doing quite poorly." The children were solemn. It was as if a mighty animal had been felled.

On the bus ride home, Elliot asked the driver to stop twice. Only when he was outside the vehicle would a child cry, softly, "Mr. Brock is puking!" And they all were shocked. There was silence when he returned, sweaty faced.

Elliot sat next to Danika for the ride home, without speaking much. Danika was a bold girl and taller than most, but she did not speak either. She wore a yellow t-shirt and red knee-length shorts, and she had some marker colouring on her arms, like a child playing with tattoos. Elliot was remote.

"Are you okay?" she asked him.

"I'll be fine, Danika," he said. "Thank you for asking. Although I'm not so great right now, it will pass." He was leaning back into the seat bench.

"Okay," she said, going back to the window.

They were on the highway for about twenty minutes when he spoke again.

"You have any brothers or sisters, Danika?"

"Yeah, I got a sister," she said.

"Oh, that's right. Younger sister." His eyes were still closed, head resting back.

"Yeah, Lasia. She's seven."

"You take care of your sister?"

Danika blanked, unsure of the question. "What?"

"If other people are mean to Lasia, do you stand up for her?"

Danika thought about this, pushing out her lips. Last year she had shoved her sister at school. There had been a spat over a ball game the older children had been playing. Lasia had fallen down and cried, and later Danika cried as well. Her parents had been told about it, and she had gotten in trouble. The girls had gone home, quietly, holding hands.

"Yeah," she said. "I stand up for my sister. I like my sister."

"That's good. I'm glad."

Elliot was lying back, drained empty and letting his limbs rest heavily in the seat, his head rolling slightly outward into the aisle of the bus. The children were noisy again with talk of animals and outbursts between groups. A perpetually yelling boy was yelling at a girl about something she had said, insisting that it was wrong. Elliot did not intervene. We were getting closer to the school, and he turned to Danika.

"I should've quit those fries," he said. "You should never accept a food dare."

Danika nodded, serious.

"Something like that is not going to end well. I promise you." His eyes were closed.

A few minutes later, he opened his eyes and rolled his head toward the window. "She's going to laugh at me when I get home," he said.

Danika did not know how to respond to anything he was saying so she played with a bead bracelet around her wrist, rolling the beads around with her finger, something she did sometimes in class.

"Will you promise me you will not accept a food dare?"

"I promise, Mr. Brock," she said, solemn.

"You won't suffer for your pride?"

"I promise I won't."

The children were recognizing the roads back to school, and the noise was dimming—everyone was exhausted, surrendering to their return, to the end of the day.

"Last thing," Elliot said. "Do not eat from a skinny woman with a mean face."

DINNER

MARTIN ARRIVED HOLDING A MAGNUM BOTTLE of white wine and wearing a poorly fitting shirt. It had been raining earlier that evening, and he was lightly spattered on the shoulders. He was a tall man, lumpy-bodied, awkward, but determined and gregarious.

Ellie thanked him for the bottle, feeling immediately bad for his cheap shirt. She turned the bottle in her hands to read the label politely. Tom came down the hallway toward the door, brushing his hands lightly on his arm sleeves and giving Martin a firm shake. "Good to see you," he said brightly. Martin asked if he was early. "Not at all," Tom said. "A few are in the back."

"I think this bottle is for him," Ellie said after Martin made his way to the backyard to join the others. "I think it's opened."

"Put it in the fridge; he can have it," Tom said.

Everybody was drinking and talking about movies, then television. Dishes from the dinner were filling the sink already. Ellie had arranged this dinner a month earlier, thinking about it frequently each week, planning and wanting it to be good. It seemed to be going well so far. She heard her own voice clipping higher with each glass of wine and watched her husband from a distance as he grew more animated, more intimate. He was typically reserved with guests. He was describing a hockey game and, according to his emphasis, making an argument for something. Ellie had a basic and dutifully broad understanding of key sports issues and had probably heard his speech before—but as always she found she could not care.

Tom was a compact, solid man, straightforward in movement and appearance, with a wide, uncomplicated face. His dark forearms curved out of the shirt cuffs he had rolled up. She remembered him vigorously peeling an orange, those dark forearms working, shortly after they had first met—a memory that returned to her over the years. She contemplated some of these elements while listening to the sound—but not the words—of him talking.

His voice made her feel restless; Ellie got up and walked around the yard through the damp grass. She called back occasional remarks to the group, feeling tipsy and brushing her hand along the leaves and tops of flowers. It was a cool night, and some of the leaves were damp. She heard a sputter of laughter coming from her dinner guests and a rise in voices. She tugged on a thick leaf to see if it would break free, but it held firm.

The backyard reminded her of her childhood. She grew up with two orange cats, both boys. Slinky animals that were affectionate but also absent, preferring to walk around in the park behind their house rather than play with her. Her house now had a park behind it too, beyond the yard, except there was no gate and the fence was only chest-high. Bushes ran along the fence, not very tall, and she was always vaguely disturbed but intrigued by the possibility that anyone in the park could stand against that fence, perhaps leaning on it with their arms, and look into her backyard. In the nighttime, it would be impossible to see a person doing that. It was too dark in the back, but she and her guests were close to the house, lit up softly like ghosts.

Her attention returned to the group—a friend of hers from work was telling a story about a house party she had held some time ago. She wandered back to the party, drying her hands on the skirt of her pale dress.

"She wasn't really supposed to drink. I didn't know that, so you know we had all of our liquor out, and white wine, and of course she was drinking. It was the medication she was on, antidepressants I think, and she just got so drunk so fast. I didn't even see it happening, really; it was just instant. So the rest of the night we were trying to take care of her. We put her on the sofa, but she rolled off and smashed the coffee table"—laughter—"but we didn't know she had been sneaking off to the bathroom with the bottle of vodka.

"I mean, I thought she could barely walk. But she was hiding with the vodka; she managed to get to the bathroom and lock the door."

Ellie winced. The story was shared with good humour and some sympathy, but she had her own humiliating stories involving drinking—Tom would know that, too. He was smiling along with the anecdote.

She liked this woman, mostly, but it was an effort to deflect small pangs of jealousy with her husband around. Allison had long hair that she was attentive to, flipping it around every so often, an appealingly luxurious self-adjustment she performed with ease. She was fit, upbeat, funny. She had left her husband last year, for vague reasons that sounded like boredom. And she was four or five years younger, still enthusiastic about everything. Ellie was conscious of it all, cool-eyed, trying to avoid getting involved.

"Finally we got her in a car, sent her home. The bottle of vodka was gone—I mean, gone. And Monday at work she didn't remember anything. Not even the coffee table. She had smashed through the glass top, couple inches thick."

"Ah, poor woman," Rachel said, sensing more laughter ahead. Rachel was a quiet person, with shoulder-length dark hair and a round face. When she smiled, she looked like a child—still kept a few gentle freckles across the top of her nose and cheeks, still had curly hair. Ellie had met her during a volunteering phase a half decade ago.

"Yeah," Allison said. "We weren't really close; it was an invite I put out online."

"Drunk guests, what a mess," Ellie said loudly, getting up. "Can I get another round for anyone else?"

There was some laughter. Tom smiled.

"Bring me something," Martin said, his voice a bit husky.

She went to the bathroom, slightly unsteady on her feet but regaining herself after slipping her feet out of her shoes, feeling her bare feet on the cold tile. She looked searchingly in the mirror. After a couple of drinks, she would have these moments in the bathroom. I feel good; I look good. The food was okay. Allison's kind of an asshole, isn't she? Making fun of that woman? Or just normal. Nevertheless—the show goes on.

She came out of the bathroom and rummaged through the carved wooden box on the coffee table, tapping out a pinch of weed into her pipe, sparking and inhaling, then releasing a long, elegant exhalation. She admired it drifting across the room. She slipped on her shoes, pulled a bottle of white out of the fridge, and headed to the backyard, gripping the bottle by the neck, feeling her body moving through the darkness, light and easy.

Her smile at Martin was an exaggerated version of a real smile. “Here ya go.” She handed him the bottle.

“Here I go,” he said happily.

It was a warm night. The air off the lake had a heavy green scent; Ellie sensed it even at a distance. She sat down with the guests. She suddenly felt very calm, sipping her wine and blinking slowly into the glass. Someone had been talking about children, about making them believe they were special; it was a talk they had seen about parenting. The conversation briefly fell quiet.

“I first thought I was special because of a drawing of a monarch butterfly that I did at school,” Ellie started, a little quiet.

Everyone looked at her.

“I was so careful at it. I was only seven, but I made this exquisite drawing that shocked my family and my teacher. Kind of shocked me too, honestly. It won a prize at school; they said I was talented.”

She could see Rachel’s eyes as two circles of dark glass. Tom’s hands rested in his lap.

“You know, I kept trying, and for another decade or so I kept drawing, kept trying, watching and waiting to see my talent develop. See it bloom. I was hoping—I wanted it to kind of envelop me, carry me toward ... some *thing*, some kind of success. Lift me up and out of my life.

“But it never really happened. I took art classes and met a few real talents. People who were actually special. I was just trying hard; that was obvious." Her voice rose a little bit, with humour. "And they were—the actual artists—they were dishevelled, weird, you know, poorly dressed. Ugly. And, well, when I went off to school, I was more interested in getting drunk and getting laid."

A few people laughed.

"So I didn't care," Ellie said. Allison's head was cocked, her long earring swung gently, and the metallic glints winked at Ellie. "But you know, I really missed it too. Thinking I was special and that I could be."

Martin was sitting forward in his chair, his mouth turned down.

"I never thought I was special," he said.

She smiled at him, a little sadly. Of course he didn't. As a young woman, she always spoke as if she knew what she was talking about, flirted, bluffed, lied, whipped up long threads of charm around herself, thinking she might be. Someone like Martin was a child almost, without comprehension and too eager, not even knowing how to define things, let alone embody them.

"Like actors' children," Allison said. "You know, they have money, their parents are rich and famous—but they're all cokeheads. DUIs, rehab."

"Starved for specialness," Tom said.

Rachel finished her wine glass and lit a cigarette, smiled. "Yeah, but our Ellie isn't a rich kid smashing up cars."

"No, definitely not rich." Ellie, stung, finished her glass briskly.

"I think it's important to feel like you have something to give the world, to offer it," Rachel said. "And, you know, seeing other people—having it mean something to other people."

"It's a conversation," Alec said. "Artists feel like they're communicating with the world, that it has meaning."

"Yeah, I've heard that too," Ellie said. "But I don't remember thinking that. I remember wanting to be special."

A few laughed again.

"It's our generation," Allison said. "Everybody wants to be famous."

"Again, not famous," Ellie corrected. "Special."

She envied the cigarette Rachel was finishing, hearing her exhale, remembering that throat of smoke, how it used to make her feel old while she was still young. Now it would be reversed.

For some reason it was always like this. Drinking around other people, the loneliness of other people, suddenly remembering things from long ago, nostalgia and longing—more than when she was actually alone with her thoughts. Brushing against their lives, feeling the immediacy of hers.

When she was young, living in a tiny room in the city, she used to spend hours sitting at the window of her apartment, smoking, looking at the apartment buildings facing hers in the street, and the distant ones in the skyline. That stretch of sky turned orange, then pink rising into purple, sunsets and seasons fading into new colours and then, inevitably, back again. And somewhere in one of those glittering buildings, her mirror. In the form of a man. Someone who sat and watched for her, as she watched for him—and she waited for it to one day change her life. She waited for when she could finally give up what she felt was her duty all this time—to manage the shrill, daily tedium in the hopes that something beautiful would unfold. And that thing, she believed, would be a man. She was more or less raised in a world that always gestured that way—finding the other, completion—and on that thin rope she had hung all the years of her life.

If she'd had a daughter, she never would have let her do the same.

Leaning out of her chair, Rachel tapped out the cigarette on the ground. Of all her habits, Ellie associated smoking with so much of her time as a young woman, with living alone—more than the drinking, even. The red ember winked at her before it disappeared.

"I wanted to be a hockey player when I was young," Tom said.

/ / /

She didn't like to masturbate, but she did it once in a while. It never felt right, though, to watch something dirty—always with at least two men—and get it over with, and then spend three days kind of avoiding remembering whatever it was she had to watch, always so unpleasantly detached from what lust meant to her.

Lust, of course, was everything. It was better than love, that sickly, panicked thing. Lust was straightforward, but it was temporary, and that diminished its importance to most people. But not to her. Lust was like a clean blade—no tearing. And it didn't lie.

There was another man, three years ago this June.

But she had run away. Two months after that, she was in a restaurant when she felt a quiet panic overtaking her—excusing herself to the bathroom, she sat in the stall, hyperventilating, face wet, choking on it. She never contacted him again. It took her this long to hide from the shame, and then face it, and accept it, and begin the slow, unravelling process of longing for the next one. Now thirty-nine, she thought there was maybe only one or two left in her. This idea—of a man—was wounded but not dead.

/ / /

Tom was in the kitchen when she came out of the bathroom. "Are you high?" he asked.

"Yeah, a bit, from earlier," she said. "Why, is it noticeable?"

"For me, sort of. You have that dreamy voice," he said. "Getting pretty candid."

"Okay," Ellie said, entering the kitchen with him and opening the fridge. "Pretty candid?" she mused. She pulled out a bottle of wine. "I would blame the alcohol more for that."

She began to leave, but he caught her wrist. She turned and faced him as he slowly pulled her in. They stood facing each other as he pulled her hand up between them, encircling her wrist with his first two fingers and thumb. He held her wrist like that, tightly locked.

"Alcohol makes you friendly," he said. "Not necessarily candid."

"I'm getting older," she said. "The facade crumbles." Then she smiled. "And I'm starved for specialness."

He looked at her, reading her face. She had a long face with a sensitive mouth in the middle, full lips often pinched in one expression or another, and eyes that never seemed fully open, as if making something out from a distance. She didn't make eye contact often; she preferred to glance away to speak or listen. He held her wrist.

"I'm not going to let go," he said.

"Oh, were you looking for a kiss?" she asked.

"Sure," he said.

Her eyes went a little cold, but he did not perceive it.

"Later," she said. And she offered him another smile. "When we're good and dead."

He was appeased, and she slipped out; he followed with another beer.

Outside, Martin was drunk. Ellie felt a little embarrassed by Martin, but also protective, sensitive to some weakness they shared. He was a large, awkward man, always last to go home. And she remembered well her early years, when she was the person in the room who stayed too long, drank too much, waiting to be welcomed and known.

They were sitting in large wooden lawn chairs in the backyard after darkness had fallen, thick. Alec had already left; he was a friendly, outgoing man in her department at work who had been quiet that night. Rachel chain-smoked for about half an hour, talking less, perhaps a bit drunk, then said she had to go home. Allison stayed for a while after that, talking about a long hike in Ecuador that seemed particularly arduous, part of her listing of vacation spots. Eventually she left too.

The backyard chairs were throne-like. Tom had picked them out, something a man is keen to own when he has bought some land and found a woman. Tom, Ellie, and Martin sat there, drinking. Martin's face gleamed in the dim outdoor lighting; his voice was quieter now, but steady.

"I had to go to San Diego for work," he said. "We had a working group down there; we were launching a new sales office in California, and one of our founders had been living there for twelve, thirteen years already. I went down there and helped the team set up. I had helped hire two of the people—one woman we stole from another firm, but anyway.

"On the fourth day, the founder guy came in and introduced himself. He spent the afternoon with the new team—a small group, but we were expecting big growth early—and then invited me and one of the senior hires to dinner, so just three of us.

"It was an unbelievably expensive restaurant—the guy paid for it all, obviously—I think some bottles were like a grand at least. And the founder got drunk. Didn't surprise me; I had heard he was a drinker. His wife had died some years back. He got drunk at the dinner and then invited both of us back to his estate, overlooking the Bay. Of course we went—I wanted to see where this guy lived. A black car that I'm pretty sure was a vintage Bentley picked us up and took us back."

Ellie felt, somehow, that the story would end in a melancholy way. Martin's voice was languid, dreamy.

"So he shows us his place; it's this sprawling property right on the Bay. We're looking at the Pacific Ocean, the largest and deepest ocean in the whole world—he tells us that. He's pretty drunk, and he's showing off. And he gets to showing us the dolphin."

Martin paused, taking his time to pour another glass for himself and gently set the bottle down. Tom and Ellie were quiet.

"We walk to the back of the house, and there's this perfect blue oval in the ground; it's a pool, but in fact it's only the outdoor portion of the pool—the rest is indoors—and it turns into an indoor pool in a kind of adjoining space, part of the house." Martin became a little unsure, trying to describe the pool. "It's like a huge tank, some of which is indoors, some of which is out," he says, gesturing with his arms. "It's bigger than you can imagine."

"And he tells us her name, Ginny. 'So this is Ginny,' he says to us. And then he explains—Ginny was actually the name of his wife who died some years back. She had loved dolphins, and so there we were. He had a dolphin."

"Is that legal?" Tom said. "People can own dolphins?"

"I don't actually know, really, but it seems kind of wrong. I mean, this animal, its intelligence, in a tank instead of the ocean"—Martin was growing agitated—"but it wasn't a wild dolphin; he got her from—from somewhere—"

"Okay," Tom said. "What was Ginny doing?"

"She was swimming in the indoor portion, and she saw us."

"She saw you," Ellie said.

"She came out to the outdoor pool, and she was looking at us. It's so quiet, up high on the Bay, overlooking the ocean, and really the only sound was the rippling of the pool. Which is very quiet, actually, like a hush."

Martin stopped speaking, and no one said anything.

The moon was out. A high, bright circle, it was up behind Tom's head, in a small clearing between the branches of the neighbour's tree, framed perfectly from where Ellie sat. But she didn't contemplate it; she was waiting.

A pop and a hiss—Tom opened another beer.

"So you met a captive dolphin," he said.

Martin nodded in the dark. "A rich guy's dolphin, named after his dead wife."

"I wonder what she would have thought," Ellie said, "of a dolphin living there, named after her."

"I don't think she would have been crazy about it," Tom said.

"She was beautiful," Martin said. "Tipped her head out of the water; I saw her face and eyes. I tell you, never looked at them so close. You look at them in the eyes, and somehow, I don't know, you feel less human. Like, you feel you have less understanding, like she knows things you don't know, if that makes sense." Martin took a drink. "Probably she does."

Ellie and Tom were looking at Martin; it was quiet.

"Not that he was the loneliest bachelor," Martin said. "In that income bracket, there are always girlfriends, or friends, or whatever. But getting the dolphin; I don't know. There's lonely, and there's millionaire-lonely, and I guess there's millionaire-who-gets-the-dolphin lonely."

"Millionaire-anything isn't so bad," Tom said.

"And the other hire that was with me, she barely spoke the rest of the night. I don't know if she was drunk necessarily, just speechless. Hardly said a word."

"Well, really, what is there to say?" Ellie stood up. She felt unsteady. "Bathroom for me."

She walked into the house, packed the pipe tightly, took another deep haul, and released a soft grey cloud—it gently pulled apart, moving away from her.

She walked through the smoke and out the front door.

/ / /

Last November. She had smoked too much and was way too high, watching a hockey game with Tom. The ice was so white, the players gliding in and out of frame like dark fireflies in a white sky, leaving a trail. Close-ups of people's faces, screaming. Children's faces, screaming. An advertisement for a vehicle skidding in slow-motion through a desert, sending up flames of sand. Is this normal? she wondered. Or am I just too high. These people do not seem normal. And she looked over at Tom, passive on the sofa.

A powerful moment passed over her, like a cloud over an open field.

This is his whole life.

Tom was only going to get older. That was all he was going to do. He wasn't going to wander or forget himself or suffer without knowing why, wasn't going to ask why, probably ever. He would have physical changes, and one day his body would fail him, hers also; they would do that together. But she was going to be alone in facing her life. She felt she was watching it like finely sifted grains; all the details were there, and counted. He didn't see it at all.

She saw the opportunity to shift away. Not in a way that he would notice, but within herself, a rearrangement of feathers that composed a new bird. New colours that appeared at dusk.

She realized she had been lying awkwardly on some pillows, so she sat up. Her arms were numb. Coming back to life, they started to ache.

/ / /

She hardly felt drunk. She had gone around the house and was in the park, heading toward the tracks.

Above the park, a steep embankment led up to a tall fence, nine or ten feet high, and beyond that a sharp but short cliff, maybe around five feet deep. And then there were the train tracks. Commuter trains hammered those tracks all day, three times an hour, more during rush periods. Standing up on that embankment, she would be able to see the neighbourhoods to the south and west, the empty stretch of grass that lined the bluffs, and then the lake. The long white face of the moon across the black body of water. She did things like this while drunk—leaving restaurants to stand on the sidewalk, sneaking out of her yard to look at the moon, smoking a stolen cigarette on the curb, watching cars, wondering if anybody interesting was inside them. And then coming back, distracted—lighter. Fresh air, detours, something she could do alone.

The fence was cut open—that was new—so she slipped through the opening.

The grass was still damp, and she stepped through muddy clumps of slick earth that felt cold beneath her shoes. She felt angry with Tom but was unsure why, an occurrence that was happening more and more often. She imagined he would not miss her much if she died first. She was somehow necessary to him, but not important. She saw herself too—a well-accommodated wife, barren but kept and cared for, walking a reliable path to the end of her life. There was a distant vibration, and she turned to look; a train was coming from the east. She felt this would satisfy her somehow. It would be loud, shake the ground, thrill her. Through the fence, she had a better view of the quiet lineup of rooftops, the bluffs, the water—but the muted scene felt cold to her tonight. The houses, the lives in the yellow squares of light, unimportant. The train defied it all.

Poor Martin, she thought. Poor me. Poor rooftops all crowded together but lonely; you are just like me, except in bedrooms. Poor moon, pointless. Because it's more than loneliness, isn't it? It's a boredom that shakes you loose. A distraction from meaning, that elusive thing all these years—that undying myth. Strangers were gifts, giving it new life. But poor lust, spat on. We were all lying. We found homes, but we were still strays.

The train was getting closer, and she watched it, a circle of white light, and she stepped carefully, watching.

She had the thought a mere half-second before it happened—what if the train saw me? would they think I was jumping? what if I slipped—and she slipped.

Her legs slid away from her and down, spinning her to the side and then flipping her over; her stomach hit the earth, and her body slid down the sharp drop to the gravel floor. Her knees crashed on the gravel, hard. The suddenness dumbed her more than the pain, or the drunkenness; she struggled to understand the abrupt twist of reality and her new position in it. The train was getting louder—but she knew she would not be hit.

She stood, briefly, to gauge whether she should try to climb up. Two or three rough clamours did nothing except drag more mud down around her. She quickly crouched and huddled against the wall of the short cliff—the train was releasing a dooming peal of sound. She cowered into the wall, her face against earth, her arms wrapped around her head, covering her ears.

The train tore past, sending gravel spraying against her arms and bare lower legs. The shaking roar consumed her, and before it was too much, before it shattered everything, it broke and it was gone. The horn sounded again, sounding mournful this time, like it did from a bedroom window—something like distant, lost whales. Then it fell quiet again.

Ellie stood up. Her dress, arms, legs, and face were slick with mud. She made grim, determined attempts to crawl up the short cliff in the soft earth, succeeding after some time, flat on her stomach and grabbing and kicking, struggling like a turtle.

She found the gap in the fence and walked down the embankment, toward the park. Upright again, she walked stiffly. An older woman stood in the park with a small dog that was circling a patch of grass, preparing to squat. Ellie did not look directly at the woman but she sensed the face turning to follow her.

/ / /

Tom could scan and read her face the way a farmer looks for rain. Thirteen years of passing moods trained him to see the next few hours in a careful review of her eyes and mouth, which hid nothing, sitting open like two palms. Without cleaning herself up, Ellie went straight into the backyard, and Tom met her two wide, white eyes in her muddied face with the same searching look.

"Holy shit!" Martin said, half-rising from the lawn chair. "Ellie! What happened?"

"Ellie—" Tom said, but didn't finish.

"I fell down," she said, walking over to them and sitting in her chair. "I slipped, slid down. I was walking around the hill above the park."

"Near the tracks?" Tom asked.

"Yeah." She was still stunned, subdued. She was looking straight ahead, not at either of the men.

Martin sat down in his seat again. "Are you okay? You know, you are—you're covered in mud."

"Yeah, I know," she said.

She picked up her glass of wine; some of the soil was starting to dry and flake off her fingers. She didn't wipe her mouth before tipping the glass against her lips. "I fell down."

/ / /

She was married for another two years, which was a lot, she felt. The man that caused its end didn't last very long either; soon she was alone. She adopted a sleek grey cat and named it Ginny, a private joke to herself, because shortly after the night she came home covered in mud, Tom posted a story about it so that their friends could laugh—the drunk wife.

She lived in a building with the cat. She was on the fourth floor, which she loved—seeing people on the street from not too high up, catching words, seeing their white sneakers at dusk. She worked in a nearby daycare as an administrator—a position well below her experience, but a place where she felt she could go unnoticed for a year or more. She didn't socialize much, but she still drank, watching movies and eating in the evenings. There was a man in the building that she looked at, but he was married to someone pleasant enough. All the men coming to the daycare were young fathers. Mostly she watched the children. She was bored, but not unhappy.

She awoke one night in the elevator. She was drunk, couldn't remember how or why she got there. She was wearing only a nightshirt; she smelled urine. She walked, poorly, back to her apartment. She changed her nightshirt and pulled on underwear and got back into bed, scared. Ginny jumped up and lay nearby, looking at her and then around the room, unconcerned.

THE ARTIST

SHE DID HER SHORT HAIR IN SPIKES, mostly upwards on the top of her head, a few sideways, the rest slicked down with heavy gel. It looked all right. She was wearing a purple t-shirt and the purple pants she had seen in the thrift store window, giving her the whole idea in the first place. He had worn all purple in his last music video, and his hair had been like this. After buying the pants in the window, she was suddenly thrust forward with new energy, thinking fast, especially at night waiting to fall asleep.

She came out of the bathroom and her father, on the sofa, had the TV on but was looking at his phone. He didn't work much in the winter.

"Okay, Dad, I'm going."

"How'd the hair come out?" He turned around halfway, then jerked his body further to see better. "It looks good, right?"

"It looks okay."

"The pants are big though, eh?"

"Yeah," she said, looking down at the fabric bunching around the belt.

"Still looks good though."

"Okay I'm going now."

"Have fun, Carrot."

She walked to school without a hat, the sharp wind cutting through her gel-damp hair. Her scarf was wrapped around the lower half of her face to compensate. She walked alone, eventually catching up to smallish groups of kids, passing them. Inside, crowds of kids peeled off coats in the noisy, steaming halls. They had half a day first; he was coming in the afternoon.

She went to class without talking to anyone, although a few kids stared at her spiked hair. She didn't talk much anyway; she had overcome a mild speech impediment a few years back but was still slow to speak up. It was unclear if the shyness had caused the speech problem, or the reverse. She sat at her desk, and the tall boy next to her looked at her twice.

"Is that for the assembly?" he asked.

"Yeah," she said.

His face was flat, unimpressed.

/ / /

She remembered first hearing his music in the car. She didn't remember where they were driving, but she remembered empty fields, so it must have been out east past the low-slung industrial buildings, where land started stretching out. She was riding shotgun. His song came on the radio, and as trees and fields slid past her window, she felt lifted up, suddenly older. The fields outside the car were more vivid now. She didn't fully understand the lyrics, but she knew he was saying he was alone—and she sensed something else when she saw his videos: he was proud, too proud to not be alone. That was something new for her. Alone was the feeling she knew and where she was safe, but she rarely felt happy. When the view outside her window turned back to low houses on wide lots, then upright houses tight together, and then the apartment complex where her building clustered with the others, it was already dusk. She wanted to hear the song again. An ember cooled inside her; the warmth was leaving.

Soon she had found out he was a local artist, and less than a year later—when he was huge, when he started touring big cities around the world—she found out he had gone to her school. It was immense to her; it was fated. A golden light turned and rested on her small life, illuminating everything.

Now he was visiting their school and they were having an assembly in the gym. All the children sat cross-legged on the floor for the short visit, necks whipping around whenever the doors opened.

First three men entered the gym wearing fat winter coats, looking around at the children and then looking at each other. And then he came in, followed by two women. He wore a leather jacket on top of a black hoodie pulled up over his head. He looked around the room, rubbing his hands.

They talked among themselves, then briefly with two teachers and the principal, and then the principal came to the front of the gym where a microphone was standing. "I remember this young man from almost ten years ago," she started.

He was standing to the side, listening. He had pulled his hoodie down.

"—Europe, Asia, South America—now he's been all over the world, sharing his music. And he's come here to share his dream with us today." The principal started clapping; everybody else did too.

He came up to the front of the assembly, hands up, palms open; the clapping rose up to a roar, and the kids stood up, cheering. Teachers rushed in from the sidelines and tried to bring them down. The gym teacher started blowing his whistle, waving his arms. The children were settled down to a simmer.

He leaned close to the microphone, his voice soft. "Hey everyone."

The room erupted again.

As all the children rose and cheered, she stood up and watched. She was lost in the crowd. Her hair and purple clothes, they disappeared—she realized suddenly how her outfit, her little attempt, would be invisible. Dressing earlier this morning, she hadn't known that yet. Buying the pants, she hadn't seen it. But now it settled on her: in the middle of a crowd, invisible—it was familiar. He wouldn't see.

The disappointment fell heavily at first. She watched him over the heads of all the other children in front of her; she felt the noise at her back. But the feeling drifted away as she saw him standing up there alone.

It was so strange—he was shy. In front of a room of children, his voice was still soft and shy. From arenas to this. First he talked about growing up in the area and walking to school through the park everyone walked through; he mentioned the chicken and pizza place where lunch was $3.99 with a pop. The room roared at everything. His face shone, and he drank a few times from a metal water bottle jutting from his jacket pocket. He told everyone to stay in school and work hard and find something they love to do. "It's not easy—this is not easy," he seemed to say about himself, but he trailed off.

She tried to imagine him walking through that park or getting a box of wings, and she could not see it. It was blank, unreal in her mind. But she saw him now very clearly, from deep in the crowd—how shy he was. Again she felt that gold light turn on her.

Then he took questions. The kids stood up; most had pieces of paper, but a few just rambled their questions at him. His answers were patient but short; he did not talk at length. He seemed to drift off and not really find it again. She had a question prepared and folded up in the pocket of her purple pants, but when she felt like standing up and asking it—imagining the room falling quiet and his eyes on hers—her heart failed her, beating too painfully. She would stumble. And her question hardly made sense, not in this room; yet it was the only thing that had come across her mind, sitting with the pencil and paper. The one thing she wanted to know, vague and behind all the other things.

And then everything was over.

He was waving, walking away. The teachers were waving the kids down; the principal came up to the microphone again while he was walking down the length of the gym. He left.

The kids quieted; teachers started asking rows to stand up and leave, starting at the back. It had only been about twenty minutes, but something had shifted in her—how shy he was against the chaos of the crowd. She remembered the question folded up in her pocket.

"You wearing that because of the music video?" a girl asked, from an older grade, sitting behind her, as they stood up and waited to file out.

"Yeah," she said.

/ / /

Her scarf was up around her face. The excitement of the day was fading now, and as she left the school the snap of cold air brought her back to her life. The sky was grey, without clouds or sun, just the same grey everywhere.

He was so shy, even after the big stages in those faraway cities. He must be rich now; he must know he never had to worry about what everybody else here was worrying about. He'd escaped. Was free. Was loved—cheering kids, roaring crowds. Yet it was not enough to make him bold; his voice was still soft in the microphone, reaching out, unsure. His songs, still empty of people, still alone.

She was walking home behind the grocery store, cutting through the back lot when she saw them. Two tall, black SUVs were parked in the far back corner.

Her step slowed, and she changed her direction slightly to avoid them, even though she was aiming for the break in the fence and the path into the neighbourhood of towers where she lived. She didn't want to walk close to those cars.

As she moved across the lot, she saw three men standing in thick coats. They were on phones. And then she saw him, sitting on the curb with a woman standing over him. His head was hanging. His hood was pulled up.

Her breath caught in her chest, and it shot down her body, her step staggering with the recognition. She stopped in the middle of the lot.

The men looked at her, and the woman turned too.

For a moment nothing happened. Then, from the curb, he lifted his head and saw her. He gestured up to the woman and they exchanged a few words—the woman seemed unwilling, but he was still gesturing with his hand.

"Hey," the woman called out. That was all she said.

She pulled her scarf down but didn't say anything, walking a few more steps but turning slightly toward them. *Me?* she gestured.

The woman waved her in.

She walked up, her heartbeat sending tremors down her legs. He was sitting on the curb, knees apart and elbows on his knees. He lifted his head and looked at her.

"Hey. You from the school?"

"Yeah," she said. Her voice was small. She was fully automatic, unthinking, watching herself dumbly from a distance.

"You dressed up? Like the video." He gestured to her hair and the purple pant legs at the bottom of her coat.

The closest SUV opened, and a second woman climbed out.

"I thought I saw that." His head dipped suddenly, and he looked at the pavement before regaining himself. "In the gym. In the assembly."

The girl nodded, not finding any words.

"Hey, we shouldn't sit out here," the second woman said. "In public," she added.

"If I get back in the car now, I'll be sick," he said. His head hung low again. The shine on his face, his low-lidded eyes—the girl realized he was drunk. It made her uneasy; she knew her father this way. Elbows on his knees, she saw his hands were bare and looked tight with cold. He looked up at her. "I've been sick a long time. I started that shit early." Then he said to the woman, voice lowered, almost apologetically, "We're just talking."

But the woman persisted, now turning to the girl. "You live near here? Walking home? You should probably go now; he's not feeling well, okay? Okay, honey?"

The "honey" at the end was cold to the girl; she felt it like a shove. Everybody was looking at her. She mumbled and started to turn away.

"Hey, hey—wait a sec." He stood up. "We're just talking. You like music? You going to be an artist?"

Her face flushed with confusion as he rose up and stood in front of her, almost unsteady. He was not tall and still lean like a teenager. There was an overhang in his shoulders left over from shielding his young frame from the world—maybe other kids hadn't liked him, she thought. Maybe someone in his family was mean. His face seemed older than his body with deep lines around his mouth; she saw a scar from his lip to his chin she hadn't noticed in his videos.

But she was overwhelmed—no one would believe this; she couldn't even believe this. He was standing here, asking her questions, drunk, looking into her face.

"I can't play any music," she said.

"You like my music?"

"Yeah."

"Why?"

No one would believe this. She struggled with words. Moments were hailing down on her, and she flinched against everything.

"Why," she said back to him.

"Yeah. Why do you like my music."

"Because," she said. "I don't know. Because I thought—I feel like we're the same, almost." Her face was hot. "Your music—you seem alone."

"Yeah." His eyes softened. "Alone."

"I feel like that sometimes." She was trying to make sense.

"Yeah."

His shoulders dropped, and he looked at her simply. "Funny thing is you never get ahead of it. Not really. Shadow's always on you."

She didn't fully understand the words but read his expression—exhausted but simple, like relief.

"Hey," one of the women said softly.

"Yeah, public, I know," he said to the woman.

He looked back at her.

In her mind he would have opened his arms and offered her a hug and for a moment she would have disappeared into it. It would be dark and quiet in there.

But in that parking lot he looked at her, drunk, nodding but somewhere else, the gleam on his face fading. And he didn't have any words left.

One of the men in thick coats came up to her and took her elbow. "Let's go home now," he said.

/ / /

She stumbled into her apartment where her father was asleep on the couch. He hadn't been drinking though. There were no cans—probably just weed.

She was buzzing. She went to the balcony and looked out over the balconies across from her, crowded with bikes and chairs and strings empty of laundry in the cold. Sometimes plants or a cat in the window. So many lives stacked together; it always made her feel small—she would feel this way for a long time, at school and everywhere else. But now, like a ringing in her ears, everything seemed more alive, illuminated and humming from within.

She tried to brush her hair out, but the frozen gel was brittle. She put her head into the hot shower stream and melted it off.

She towel-dried and changed into grey sweatpants and a sweatshirt, but as she was pulling off the purple pants, she felt the paper crinkle in the pocket, and remembered the question.

She took the paper out and opened it.

what will happen to me?

"I DIDN'T SEE ANY CHILDREN WITH BALLOONS"

HER HUSBAND DIED AND LEFT SOME MONEY. She sold the business—a car repair shop where she did the bookkeeping—and retired. And then she did something unusual. She bought balloons and sat on the corner, in the seat of her walker, and waited for children to walk by. And when one did, she gave them a coloured balloon, smiling, almost shyly—as if she did not know why she did this either—and the child shyly accepted it. And sometimes, if she had not seen many young children, she gave a balloon to an older child or a teenager, and they were embarrassed—some tossed the balloon quickly, others carried it awkwardly for some time. Driving the streets around the neighbourhood, you were reminded of her because you occasionally saw a small child holding a balloon—red, blue, pink—or saw one discarded in a bush. Once a balloon was waiting alone in a bus shelter, at the top. Sometimes you looked up and saw one released, floating away.

I knew her because I opened a dog-grooming business in the shopping plaza near her corner. I saw the children walking by with balloons for weeks and never knew why —until, driving by her corner one day, I noticed her sitting there with the clutch of balloons. Without thinking I tapped the brakes as I passed her, caught by the colours, and a car horn bleated behind me, annoyed. "All right, all right," I said. I sped up a little, still looking back over my shoulder at the woman, her long greying hair over a dark coat.

It had taken a long time for my business to pick up. I remembered many long hours at first, with nothing to do before I had enough regular clients—frankly it was a boring area, with a series of strip malls offering mediocre services and retail. And I remembered looking out the front shop windows and seeing the children holding balloons. So when I finally saw her, saw the round, bobbing colours, it felt as if a small mystery had revealed itself to me. The woman who owned the coffee shop in the plaza said her name was Marta.

One of my first regular clients had a nasty-looking old greyhound mix, with angry eyes set in her brindle face. That dog looked at me with real hatred. Her owner wanted me to bathe her every single week—it wasn't my fault. She was muzzled during the bath but tried to snap at me anyway, she was so angry. Frankly her attitude was just making it last longer than it needed to—which I explained to her patiently as I sprayed her down. Some dogs just didn't get it. The owner was a chatty woman, however, and talked about Marta more than once. The greyhound would stand there looking at me with those monstrous eyes, one on each side of her head like a shark, and the owner would be chatting away, flopping her hand as she talked.

I heard about Marta's husband and his business, their two daughters, how one of them died as a child in the hospital and the other one grew up and did well enough in school to get an important job in New York. Her name was Aleksandra. But she was far away now. And then Marta's husband died, and she was abruptly alone. Maybe the balloon thing made her feel less lonely. Most people agreed this was the case. And they were fond of her—a mix of pity and amusement, the kind a neighbourhood has for its eccentric. I felt a little fond of her as well. The weirdo, like me.

/ / /

My business was finally picking up after almost nine months of boredom and then a quietly growing desperation. But the clients came, and they stayed. For the next six months, I overworked myself and delayed hiring an assistant for fear the clients would suddenly disappear. Rob was annoyed with me working late every night and coming home an empty shell, opening a bottle. But exhaustion overtook me, so I hired a person to help, and finally I had a business going. My part-timer occasionally did work so that I didn't have to, and instead I emailed clients. I was sleeping longer, full nights, and my body relaxed with relief.

I kept my favourite client, a huge, heavy mutt that was halfway between an Irish wolfhound and a fat teddy bear, almost obscenely covered in thick fur that was occasionally deep grey and occasionally chocolate coloured. What a happy beast. Bison, they called him. I saw him once every two weeks, and those fourteen days in between felt long. Once his owner cancelled his appointment and I was so disappointed, I had two glasses of wine with lunch. I thought of Bison's face—a happy, round thing, split open in the middle with friendly winks of white teeth and a fat pink tongue. What a good dog.

I saw Marta throughout the week as I drove around the neighbourhood to run errands or drop off cards. One Wednesday, I was running across the street to another plaza to buy a charging cord, and I was passing her. I had changed my appointments for the day so I could catch up on receipts and the spreadsheet. I thought I might say hello.

I nodded at her, feeling almost self-conscious because I had already heard of her life but had never introduced myself. I hesitated as I passed, suddenly shy, but she spoke.

"You are even more interesting up close," she said.

Her eyes were glittering. I thought she was having some fun with me; I thought she might have meant me being gay. Some old people made a thing about it, made odd comments. But there was a rise in her voice, bracing herself for a bright response. So I said, "What would you expect from a dog groomer?"

She laughed at me. "I've never met a dog groomer, so I wouldn't know what to expect," she said. "I just saw you across the street, and I liked your cap. It's Italian. And then you got close, and I saw your shoes." She was amused so she continued, "What kinds of dogs?"

And we talked a bit about my business for a short while—I told her how I left my other job to try to start this, and how it was going so far. I even dropped a joke about my husband being the breadwinner and me being the person who tries a hobby business—a little self-deprecation I didn't usually share because I was still self-conscious about it, feeling indulged. Then I asked about the balloons.

It was a question she deflected so skillfully, with a small smile, her eyes turning a little humble: "Oh, it doesn't matter. Unless you want one?" And she put a balloon in my hand. Then she spoke of the qualities of helium—the second-most common element in the universe—and eventually concluded with a joke about humidity that I didn't fully understand.

So I walked back to my store, carrying the balloon. And I stood in my store holding it for a few moments before even realizing she had deflected my question entirely. I felt like a child, confused, standing there and holding it. A bright yellow balloon.

/ / /

Marta and I became friends and yet, months later, she still would not explain the balloons. At first she teased and deflected, and then later the question made her quiet—so I stopped asking. I remembered what the locals had told me: despite the easy and smiling eyes, she was probably lonely. And really what did my question matter—the balloons.

Marta was a woman who wasted no time becoming friendly. If she liked you, she rushed into it. Said everything. Said sad things, too. Her smile was too big, her face would easily flush with amusement, and she was tall and lean and had expressive hands that danced around when she talked. Her hands seemed to almost pantomime what she was talking about—if she was telling a story that took place during a walk, her hands would kind of run from left to right, fingers waggling like legs. If she told a story that involved picking fruit, there she was, twisting and pulling something out of the air. She seemed very young, sometimes, in a way I found difficult to describe to Rob—as if her many years had not changed anything from a plainspoken child of eight or nine. Like she was simple. Sensitive, naive, but also bold and unafraid. She liked my stories about dogs; she thought they were good people, worthy of discernment. She reminded me of an old, lean shepherd, with sagacious eyes and long, fading hair.

Not many people around my shop made an impression on me. An interesting phrase—*made an impression*. Rob used it frequently, about colleagues or clients, as if we were all soft things and other people pressed into us and left an imprint. And I liked the neighbourhood well enough for our weekly interactions: Shini, henna-haired and short, proud, busy, with the tidy coffee shop on the corner of our plaza; Bill, tall, big bellied, who owned the dry cleaner's and worked with his wife, Ina, who was small and wiry like a bird—they both seemed overwhelmed by life and work. Then there was Pri's shop with European chocolates and Turkish candies; it was a bright store, but she had sharp eyes and didn't like when people parked in the plaza and walked elsewhere. She called parking enforcement many times. I think they were quite tired of her, but she was right—there were bylaws. Pri was intimidating, well-dressed, and wore makeup every day.

They were all interesting, but none of them pressed on me. Somehow Marta, in her humble posture, in her conspicuous place on the corner, somehow she left an impression—a quietly compressed area around her.

No one else talked like her. She once described someone's heartbreak as *her heart fell like a pecan from a tree.*

Who says something like that? Unselfconsciously? I asked Rob.

Rob said, I don't think pecans fall from trees.

I said he was missing the point, but he looked it up, his face tipped down into the blue light of his phone.

Actually, yeah, he said, pecans fall from trees. In fact you are supposed to pick them up quickly so they don't rot on the ground or get snatched by rodents.

I told him Marta once said I had the face of someone who was very happy but didn't know it.

Rob considered that more thoughtfully, looking at my face.

Do I seem like someone oblivious to my own happiness? I asked him.

I do think, he said carefully, there are some things that you don't know. And then he smiled and put his hand on my arm: And I do think you are happy.

I always felt self-conscious around her—exposed. Like when a bright child says something embarrassing to you, loudly, plainly, without realizing the offence. Her eyes were kind but overwhelming. You wondered what you could keep from her, but you felt guilty about it, as if she sensed the concealment. And so I gave up on affectation. And soon I told her everything.

"Your problem," she said, "is the distance."

She had pulled down a yellow balloon and was turning it gently in front of her face, enjoying the colour, and then turning slightly to smile at me. And then she corrected herself—"Most people's problem, actually." And she considered this, her eyes straying over my shoulder.

"What distance?" I asked. We were talking about my sister and her issues with our family.

"You build this distance between how you feel, and what you do," she says. "And I'm not sure what to tell you—the longer the distance, the more tired you'll be. Exhausted, after a lifetime of it."

"But she's my sister—I can't just say these things."

It was autumn. There was a bright blue scarf around Marta's neck, high, close to her chin, and her cheeks were softly coloured in the cooler air. She wore good gloves, tight stitching around the fingers. She had half a dozen balloons left—the yellow one, and blues, reds, one green. She was not sympathetic to what I had said.

"Think about two things," she said. "One—how you feel. Two—what you do. I cannot give you advice about your sister because you already know how you feel, what you want to say, but you won't do it. You'll do something different. And you'll be reasoning to yourself, or to me, about the distance between those two things. But it doesn't matter. The distance will wear you down—in this and in everything."

She was not looking me in the face. Her hands were busy rearranging the balloons.

"Marta, do you have any sisters?" I asked.

"No," she said. Serious, and then laughing, "Thankfully."

"Well, you can't tell them what to do."

"Timothy, please," her patience was thinning. "Sisters, family, okay—customers, neighbours—people, all these people are bumping into each other, everybody drawing up distances from each other and how they truly feel, what they truly want to say or do. Between who they are, and who they are around someone else. Now, all we have—"

A child and his father were walking toward us. We saw them at the same time, and I stood back, alongside Marta's walker, to let them approach. Her mood flipped completely, and she selected the yellow balloon, holding it out.

All four of us became shy—the moment between the small boy, overwhelmed, and Marta, her face colouring deeper. The yellow balloon hung out in the air between them before his very short arm rose to reach it, the father and me watching, standing back, averting our eyes for brief moments and then looking back, hoping the two of them were happy. All of us embarrassed and confused. Finally the boy held it.

"What do you say?" asked the father. The boy looked up at him, nervous. "You say, 'thank you,'" the father said.

"Thank you," said the boy.

The father was pleased and smiled and they walked on—the small child holding the balloon and still looking at it with wonder, as if it would pull him up and away.

Marta smiled after them and then up at me.

Then she sighed. "Now all we have is this," she paused, waving her hand around at the rest of the world. "Some kind of construction—a web, complicated—of all the people we know and the distances we keep between them and ourselves. You'll get very old one day, and you'll know what I mean."

"So you want me to tell the truth to Karen? Make her cry? Make my mother upset?"

"Sure, rather than standing here, telling me—which does nothing."

She paused, thinking. Then her tone fell a bit, became quieter, softer. "If you love somebody, tell them. Tell them tomorrow. Or better tonight. Rather than spending three months lying in bed, in the dark, looking up at your ceiling. If you're angry with someone, tell them. Run into it. Don't keep this distance between you and the truth."

I was unconvinced. "Being nice, being polite, it holds all the world together. If I told Karen what was wrong with her—all the ways she ruined her life, how she upsets all of us—everything would break apart. If everybody did that—"

"Lots of things would break," Marta said.

"Everything would break," I said.

"I know," she said, finally. "That's why nobody does it. And so we carry on." She did little marching motions with her arms, the balloons gently jostling above her.

I had nothing to say to that; it was a disappointing conclusion. I was still beside her walker on the grass and we both faced the street. At the intersection cars lined up patiently and then shuffled through the lights at their turn. I didn't want to talk about Karen anymore.

"You realize"—she laughed suddenly—"you realize you're talking to the Weird Balloon Lady? Who decided, one day, *I want to give balloons to children*? And then gave balloons to children? Almost no distance there." She held up two fingers to me. "Two things, right?" She ticked down one finger: "I want to give balloons to children." She ticked down the second: "So I give balloons to children."

She sat back in her walker. "I didn't care what people thought."

"I always tried to ask why, but you ignored me," I said.

"Why is a detail only." Always deflecting. She rested her hands in her lap. "Anyway, it's liberating being the weirdo," she said. "No distance."

/ / /

It was the third week of November, a Monday, and I had a strange feeling about the neighbourhood. Looking out the windows, something was off. And then it was mid-afternoon, I was between appointments, leaning on the counter and looking out at the streets, a few people walking by on the sidewalk, and it hit me. I hadn't seen any children looking up, carrying those balloons.

I went outside, and Marta was not on the corner. I went over to the coffee shop and asked Shini, *have you seen Marta?* And she said she hadn't. Maybe she was sick.

I went back to my shop, not knowing what to do. I finished the next two appointments and caught up on emails and then locked up for the night, looking over my shoulder as I turned the key in the lock, looking at the empty corner where Marta usually sat. Rob was texting *Coming home?* and I texted back *Yeah home in 20*. Marta had not seemed sick when I saw her on Saturday.

Tuesday and Wednesday came and went—still no Marta. Children walked by without balloons. But they were my busiest days, so I was in the shop until almost seven thirty at night. Rob was impatient for me to get home for dinner. She's sick, he said, maybe you can ask around and visit her.

On Thursday Shini told me she did not know where Marta lived. More than that, she did not know who might know.

I called my client with the greyhound, and she was animated, pleased to hear from me out of the blue. "Timothy, Timothy," she said—she always said my name in twos when she was excited—but then she became sympathetic, disappointed she could not help me.

I went to Pri. Her mouth was set in a tight circle when I walked in, but she was cordial when she recognized me. *And how are you, Timothy?* I asked if she knew where Marta lived.

"Of course," she said, calmly. "Up on Dermot, 287."

I drove to the house, parked, and texted Rob where I was. I texted my assistant as well and told her I would miss my afternoon appointments. I stood outside the house for a moment—a split bungalow with a small porch, red brick, black-and-white shutters, yellow curtains, and across her lawn orange oak leaves had been windswept into small mounds. These details slowed me down. I stood on the sidewalk and looked at the house. The curtains were open.

I stepped up on the porch and rang the bell, and waited. No one came. I rang again and no one came. I walked over to the window where the yellow curtains were parted and saw, very close to the glass, a helium tank sitting next to a leather armchair, red, with little wooden feet. A sofa sat across from it, dark brown, worn and soft looking. A stone fireplace and mantle was visible from the window as well. It was overwhelming, her furniture, her photographs on the walls, her things; my mind kept pulling between all the stories she had told me and the fact that I was standing up against her window on Dermot Avenue as cars steadily drove by. But I didn't know how to leave.

A small, old man walked by with a caramel-coloured toy poodle, looking up at me from the sidewalk. The little dog was old, stiff in the hind legs. "Hospital," he said.

/ / /

I texted Rob from the parking lot. *Okay I'm sorry*, he typed back. I felt agitated but could not imagine the next step, or the one after that; everything was playing out in single scenes. I got out and went into the building. It was bustling inside; pairs and families dotted the lobby, standing and sitting and clustered in little groups around teal and beige bench seating. I was walking toward the main reception desk and stopped, cold—a child carrying a balloon—and my chest suddenly clutched into tight fists, like a heart attack. I turned suddenly to the child and her mother—"Where did you get that balloon?"—and both looked at me, taken aback, an adult man panicked for a balloon.

"The gift shop," the mother said, looking behind her. I followed her eyes and saw the stand. A small collection of four or five balloons, sitting outside the shop.

I was at reception. There were several people ahead of me. I turned and watched the girl and her mother walk through the automatic doors and toward the lineup of taxis just south of the front entrance. The light green balloon bobbed gently behind her. A little girl, about that age. It was falling on me, gently. Understanding. And like warm water, it was spreading in my chest, pooling into my arms and legs. Understanding Marta and her balloons—her other daughter, in a hospital, never coming out. Never getting the gift shop balloon on her way out.

I felt like sitting down.

A receptionist beckoned me; it was my turn.

"I'm looking for Marta. Older woman, in her seventies maybe. Or eighties," I said. The receptionist blinked at me, unsympathetic. "I don't know her last name."

"First name Marta?" he asked me. "M-A-R-T-A?"

"Yes, I think so," I said. "I know her. I just don't know her last name. Older woman, maybe seventies. Marta could be short for something else. M-A-R-T-A or something close."

He was clicking through several screens. He stopped at a screen and looked at it for a few moments, his face showing something. "Okay, can you wait?"

I said I could wait. I walked four or five feet away from the reception desk and looked out the front entrance windows. The girl and her mother and their green balloon had gotten inside a taxi. My phone vibrated in my coat pocket, but I didn't feel like pulling it out. I watched people walking in and out of the automatic doors, unable to think beyond the moment. I went and stood outside the hospital, then came back inside and stood near reception again, facing the windows.

"For Marta?"

A doctor stood in the reception area. She was looking at me, head tilted, white coat, black hair pulled back into a bun. By this point I was a little dazed, listless, eyes wandering around the lobby and out the windows—realizing how much I didn't know.

"Are you family?" the doctor asked me.

I had come all this way and didn't know the little girl's name, how it had happened. It was a cruelty against both of us, by both of us. Marta didn't tell me, and I had never asked. So all this time, she kept this distance between us—why the balloons. I looked at the doctor but faltered, could not speak. And I already knew by her face.

"A friend?" she asked. She waited, concerned, looking at my face.

"Why did you come here?"

THE DOG

THE DOG WAS OF MEDIUM HEIGHT, with a slim build and legs lean for running. Her coat was yellow with white paws; her face ended in a neat point, black-tipped, with dark little eyes set wide. She was nimble and furtive, like a fox in pale colours.

They picked her up far outside the city in a wealthy exurb; expansive, grey-bricked homes stood tall and alone overlooking wide green fields. There was some farmland here and there. She had roamed for a few days, growing hungry, eating sticks and leaves. Finally someone called a rescue group after seeing her in their yard, trying to knock over a garbage bin. A rattling pickup truck pulled slowly onto the property, and a stooped woman got out; she wore tall rubber boots heavy with dried mud. The young woman who had called stood in the doorway of her big house and called out, *Hello, I haven't seen him since yesterday, but he might still be around.* The stooped woman waved acknowledgement and went walking through the grass, looking around, then came back and took a large cage from the back of her truck. The younger woman went back into the house and watched from her window for a few minutes. Then she sat on her sofa and took out her phone; soon she heard the truck cough and choke, starting up and rumbling away.

Overnight the dog was caught.

The rescue group called her Cassie and put her on a website and sent her to live with a foster family until someone decided they wanted her. The family's home was noisy and crowded with children and dogs; the woman of the house was large and occasionally brutal, with a thundering voice to keep her children in line. Two of the children were older, brooding, sulky in their teen years; the two young ones were still boisterous and loud. Three dogs already lived there. The man of the house left early around dawn and returned in the evenings, quiet and somewhat detached from the goings-on around him. The yellow dog sat at the edges of the yard, panting softly, as the children and other dogs ran around, barking and squealing and tumbling.

She got away once.

She had been working on a quiet corner of the yard, under the fence, digging in small, unnoticed spurts. It was a creamy orange dusk in September when she cleared the underside of the fence, trotted into the neighbour's yard, without a gate, and lightly padded down the street, keeping away from cars, keeping her slim head low. The family didn't call it in, but someone saw her a week later—she was caught again. This time a van from the city picked her up; they brought her back to the large foster family. The children were happy and patted her in delirium and, a few hours later, forgot her again.

In late winter, someone wanted to adopt her. It was a young family with a toddler. Both the young husband and wife said they had grown up with dogs and they wanted one too—it would make their family complete. They had a very specific idea of how they wanted life to be and took each step one at a time, in order. They came and picked her up from the foster family and renamed her Maddie. They bought her a pink collar and a round bed in a pretty pattern that matched the living room decor. Her food dish had her name on it; her water dish was high-shine stainless steel. They patted her head and talked in high voices but preferred she did not go up on the furniture because everything was new.

The toddler had tight curls all over his head in a light brown colour. He loved the dog and grabbed at her yellow fur with fists, delighted. *Be gentle, be gentle*, his parents called out as if he understood the words. He did pause to look at them. But he grabbed the dog again, her ears, her tail, as she watched him with dark, wide eyes. She knew there was something blind about the child, that he did not understand, and she waited until he grew bored. Soon he would move to toys. Soon he would move to the sofa, pulling down the pretty pillows to the floor; his mother would come to rescue them.

The dog lived with the young family for five years. They took her on walks on a leash and did not let her loose in parks or forests; she was always, always attached. The backyard had a well-maintained fence. She ate high-quality food, and the young family posed her in photos, and their life was very well-maintained for years until the husband started drinking and the wife started messaging other men. He was trying to dull himself; she was trying to wake up. Each blamed the other for the alienation, the ennui, the vague, unrecoverable distance, and although they went to a counsellor, it was not long until it all fell apart. The ex-wife kept the little boy; the ex-husband took the dog.

He would walk her in parks, looking at his phone until he met other people with dogs, and then he chatted in a friendly way. There was a cute younger woman with a dog who sometimes came to the park, and he was very friendly with her; he offered to let the dog off-leash so the dogs could play together.

And she was gone.

///

The dog went north, moving during dusk and dawn when light was lower. Her yellow coat burned soft, like a fading ember. She moved out of the suburbs, past the wealthy enclaves and rundown outposts, out where there was space and grass and air. She did not have much to eat, but she had fattened in her previous home; she could survive. She found a wooded area and a stream for water and visited farms in the area looking for livestock feed or garbage. She stood in the fields in spring when the first butterflies moved across the tops of the grass.

Sometimes people saw her, the little scrounging dog, the pale yellow fox. A few people talked about her, but no call was made for someone to come with a cage. They thought of her as another wild thing, waited to see if she grew too thin.

She was running across a slim, dusty highway when a car hit her.

///

The driver of the car that hit her did not call it in because he thought it was a fox, not a dog. There was nobody to call for a fox. Someone found her almost four hours later after she had dragged her crushed body over to the side of the road.

A veterinary hospital wanted to put her down, but the woman that found her said she would pay. They put her through two surgeries, and she was functional—she could walk, somewhat. But it was not like before.

The dog was put up for adoption on a website for dogs with needs; she could move around, but she was stiff and sluggish. In the meantime, she stayed at another foster home with other disabled dogs. It was a cozy house with dim lighting and easygoing chaos; she did not have to run very often, and she spent afternoons in the corner on a bed. They named her Biscuit because of her yellow coat. She lived there for a full year.

An older woman found her online and said that she could care for her; she too had recovered from complicated surgeries and would not be walking much. She could take a dog; she could use the company. The woman picked her up and kept the name, Biscuit, because it sounded nostalgic and warm, like a long-forgotten home. Because she walked with a cane and the elevator in her low building was shaky, the older woman rarely left her apartment; she opened the balcony door and lay papers down for the dog to use the bathroom.

Sunsets passed by the windows high over the dog's head. Through a crack, thin threads of fresh air sometimes drifted inside. The dog had a bed in the living room and lay there all day and all night, narrow snout resting on her paws. Her dark eyes blinked soft and slow. The woman lived in a plump chair, moving sometimes between the kitchen and bathroom, nothing else. The woman had a kind heart but had given up. It seemed this is where they both would die.

/ / /

He had left the back door open briefly as he stepped inside for a small cotton rag from the kitchen. He stayed inside as he remembered all his rags were dirty already and looked for a kitchen towel instead. He had a few he didn't want to ruin, towels with little flowers, his late wife's. He searched the bathroom closet as well.

When he returned to the door with a cloth, there was a dog standing there. The dog was yellow and desperately thin, with tiny white paws that seemed to disappear on the pale wood doorstep. He was arrested by the apparition, and the sudden life in his home—he lived alone, without any pets.

"Hey there," he said softly.

Her ears turned almost imperceptibly. Her dark eyes rested on his face. He saw her hip bones poking out of her yellow coat, so he asked if she was hungry, as if she could understand. Still she did not move, but the subtle shift of her ears.

"Okay then," he said.

The widower took a few slices of turkey from the fridge, washed a carrot in the sink—the dog watching from the doorway—and put it on the floor a few feet in front of her. He retreated further into the kitchen and sat on a chair, tilting himself away.

The dog came forward and slipped the turkey quickly into her mouth, picked up the carrot, and trotted away. The man went to the door and looked out to see the slim frame glinting in the sunlight, her yellow coat lit up, luminous against the deep-coloured grass. Somewhat stiff, she moved quickly and was gone.

The widower stood for a time, feeling himself awakened and alert after a live thing had stepped briefly into his life, then left again. He looked into the woods where she had gone but did not leave his doorway. Pushing the cloth into his pocket, he sat down on the stoop. He rolled a cigarette carefully, thinking.

/ / /

Two days later, the dog appeared again. And then the day after that. And then regularly in the afternoons. She never stepped inside his small cottage but came into his yard and stood, brightly yellow, an apparition he could not fully believe and yet one that appeared again and again. If the sun tilted low in the sky and she had not come yet, he waited for her, pulling a few things from the fridge in a nervous habit, checking the windows.

The season was turning. The days were still brilliant with sun, but the evenings grew blue-black and cold. The man left the door open in the afternoons, and one day she stepped inside. She ate quickly and lay on the tiled floor, lowering her head onto her small white paws, her eyes turned away. He looked away shyly too and left the door open for hours as the small cottage grew cold with fresh air. Finally he slipped to the door and closed it. Carefully ignoring her, he went about his dinner and then to bed.

In the morning she was at the door, looking at him. There was a mournful question in her face. He opened the door; she slipped out and disappeared and was gone for three days.

But then she came back.

/ / /

They lived like that, the man and the dog. The widower left the door open, and sometimes she came in and stayed; sometimes she ate and slipped away. He learned not to worry about her the nights she was gone; he learned to trust she would come back. His old heart had broken already. Before marrying, he had preferred his freedom in solitude for many years. But then he met a woman and loved her, and much later she died, and his solitude was a sad thing now. It was without comfort, only habit. So the man held his heart aloft and safe from the dog, not wanting to turn a wild thing tame, knowing himself both ways, and knowing the pain of the latter. He knew the cost of opening your hand, letting something go; he did it anyway. He did not name her.

The dog saw something in him. He was a lean man, tall as a tree, but bent over by tiredness and time. She recognized something in his thoughtful movements around the cottage and the yard. She was old, stiff, broken too. But she had never known a home, did not know what it meant to stay, the last belonging of a heart. She looked at him, watched him, but then turned and looked to the open doorway instead. In the dark house, it was a tall opening of light.

YOUTH

THE PATH WAS NEW ENOUGH, young enough, that you had to walk with feet single file and pick your footsteps carefully between the tree roots and rocks rising out of the ground. Sometimes the branches overhead dipped low and you had to duck beneath them; sometimes the trees crowded close on either side. But the path wasn't long, and soon you were at the creek, a small clearing near the water.

After first seeing it, she didn't actually go there for a couple of months. She only looked down onto the creek from the fifth-floor balcony where she sat drinking iced tea or lemon water throughout the day. She had been a formidable drinker in her younger years, but after her husband died, her body snapped it off; she thought it might have gone the other way, two bottles a night. Forgetting to eat, losing weight. But some silent, mysterious survival instinct took over, and she could hardly have a glass of wine without feeling ill, almost overwhelmed with it. Still, she liked having a cold glass of something in her hand—tea or water—sitting alone on the balcony. Sipping and looking out.

There was a break in the tree canopy, and she could see down into the clearing. There was an ancient, heavy branch—almost a trunk in itself—slung low across the ground, and that's where the teenagers sat, smoking cigarettes and joints and drinking beer. And sometimes she saw them, a boy's white t-shirt glowing in the open space between the branches. The girls wore tank tops, had long shining hair.

More and more, she watched them from the balcony. She was retired but had worked so many exhausting years as a nurse, and then nursing her husband at the end, that she had forgotten to make hobbies or interests for herself—ways to pass time that felt worthy of a day, even just an afternoon. She struggled to fight off the sense of meaninglessness with the hobbies she tried; they were all amusing little tasks, but she could not truly care. How did people become interested, and even engrossed? Looking forward to it? And she felt that way sometimes about people, the other women at the classes, the hobby groups. Or even the women in her building, down in the lobby. She was cut off, somehow. Yet she had so much time.

The teenagers left cans and bottles around the creek. That bothered her. After a few months of watching them, she decided to go down herself, waiting until they were not around. She brought a garbage bag.

She walked through the dim path carefully and came into the clearing, a circle of sunlight resting on the ground. She looked around. There were cans and bottles at the edge of the trees, some of them filled with cigarette butts. She sat on the branch instead, still holding the bag in her hand. The creek was near-silent, clear water moving gently across the brown mud and rocks below—it was a nice place to spend time, she thought. Hang out. She thought of her husband.

She had met him late in life when his youth was well behind him, a fossilized echo of the young man he had been. She didn't know anything of his younger self, if he hung out with girls in the woods, if he ever got anywhere or only went home with longing. He had been a quiet, reserved man after a long shyness in childhood. He had been a good deal older than she was.

She stood up and started putting cans and bottles into the bag. She gathered what she thought was enough and brought it back to the building, emptying it into the recycling chute, the bottles clattering hard, the cans making thinner sounds. She put the butts in the garbage.

A month later she went again, picking up the loose ends of a restless afternoon. Weeks' worth of restless afternoons. This time she found two empty condom wrappers—different brands. At first she was horrified in that reflexive way she felt about almost anything teenagers did. But she calmed down; at least they were using condoms. When she was young, they would be parents. And then a true horror story would begin. At least they were only wrappers; the used condoms themselves were not around—cast into the river? A big finish, a final salute? Bravo, she thought. And after she thought it, she laughed out loud. Bravo!

It had been almost thirty years, and still the late-term miscarriage stayed with her as fresh and reliable as morning. Leaving that hospital with her only child left behind, cold. She thought of the teenagers like the creek, fresh water moving across an old riverbed of mud and rocks—they were always new; the path was always old. And in a way, a tender way, all of them were her children. She saw them as belonging to her somehow. But she saw them from far away.

/ / /

There was a boy she saw often by the water, and she realized he was popular—tall and lean and shoulders jutting like wings. A specimen, she thought. It was easy to recognize him because of the white t-shirts he wore, tightly. His hair was dark, his skin slightly less so—the white shirt was bright as a flag.

She started to recognize some of the girls too. Occasionally there would be another boy here or there, but it was mostly him. Sometimes he was with one girl; sometimes he hung out with a couple of them. He would be talking and they would be laughing, handing a small joint around. She felt another reflex—she didn't like him.

It was a weekend morning—Saturday or Sunday, she didn't remember. She was entering the clearing with a bag and caught her breath with surprise. A girl was there.

The girl was sitting on the branch facing away and had not seen her approach.

There was a moment to back away quietly, but she hesitated behind the girl, holding the garbage bag, looking at her back. The girl was wearing a light purple tank top and black cut-offs; she was tall and lanky, her shoulders dark from the summer sun. Her left forearm had a large tattoo—how old was she?—and she saw the tattoo as the girl lifted her arm up to her face and then back down, smoking a cigarette.

"Smoking with your left hand; that's unusual," she said to the girl. From decades working as a nurse, she knew how to disarm strangers—friendly but something unexpected and personal, something about themselves.

The girl turned around, twisting her upper body, startled. Her face was long with a thin, upturned nose. Her eyes were guarded, her mouth pulled small. There was something of a startled bird in how she looked, a lanky, long-necked bird.

"You must be left-handed then," she continued, and smiled for encouragement.

"Yeah," the girl said.

"Not many left-handed girls; it's rare."

The girl said nothing, nodding—self-conscious and uncomfortable around a stranger, even one as old as a grandmother.

"Don't mind me, I'm just picking up some trash and recycling. I live in the building; I'm retired and have nothing better to do."

The girl said nothing. She turned back around again and after a drag on the cigarette, took out her phone.

She felt a strong motherly pull toward the girl. It was an ache, both a pleasure and a pain in her body. She felt protective and fearful of the girl, with her large tattoo—how could she choose that permanence when she was so young? She would regret it. There were so many decades, so many selves, left in her life. More than anything she wanted to keep talking, but the girl would be scared off; she had to keep her here somehow.

She walked around the clearing picking up the bottles and cans and butts. The girl finished the cigarette and threw it on the ground, rubbing it out with her shoe. Then she stood up and put her phone in her pocket—she was leaving.

"That's a popular guy that comes here, eh?" Taking her eyes from the girl, she bent for two tall cans and slid them into the bag. "I see him a lot."

The girl stopped and looked her full in the face, startled again, but her guarded eyes flashed bright.

Aha, she thought.

"So you know him? Tall guy, lanky like you."

"I know him," the girl said.

She didn't know what to say next; she had struck something, and now the girl, who had been leaving, seemed to pause—unsure.

"Yeah, popular guy." She kept moving around the edge of the clearing, stooping and picking up. "He comes around here a lot with girls, sometimes in a group but sometimes one on one. Different girls."

She didn't look up but could see the girl was facing and looking at her, silent.

She kept picking up the cans and bottles. It had rushed out of her in a heedless moment; she wouldn't say anything more about it. They were both silent for a few moments.

Then the girl spoke. "I know," she said. And then, after a pause, "Sorry about the cigarette butts."

She straightened up, and they looked each other in the face. The girl's eyes were hardened; her kindly nurse authority took over. "Don't worry about it, please," she said firmly. "I'm bored; I like cleaning it up. I like the creek. I like having something to do here."

The girl seemed to smile a little, an attempt, and then left, picking her way through the narrow path and disappearing behind the branches, the tattooed arm hanging loose at her side.

/ / /

There was something pure about them, like elements. Life was long with so much sameness and repetition; life had a way of tempering you out, smoothing and polishing you down. Teenagers were pure like animals, elemental, hot and bright or dark and cold, sparking off each other, reactive and explosive. But sloppy and blind and foolish, with bravado so charming and pathetic; they were mere children who had grown too big, still smashing into things.

She remembered earlier years when she did not like teenagers, saw something cynical in that bravado. But her only child had died before birth, and it had left her so fatally humbled and longing. She saw so much wounded innocence and longing in them. And pride and vanity and struggling to pull themselves out of the bewildering madness of youth—the struggle to become someone, even only just themselves.

She still saw the boy by the creek, recognizing his height and lanky walk; they were wearing light coats now, and his white t-shirt was gone. Sometimes the groups were a mix of boys and girls; sometimes he was alone with one. She went down every month or so, gathering up what was left behind, sitting on the branch and looking at the water. Leaves were being shed and covering the ground with bright yellow and orange. She went in the morning when it was unlikely the kids would be around.

But she saw the girl one more time. This time the girl entered the clearing and she was the one sitting on the branch. She heard the crunching of leaves on the ground and turned around; they were both startled, looking at each other. She smiled at the girl with genuine warmth and relief—until, in a sharp shock, she saw the bruises on the girl's face.

The shock was brief, flickering through her, because of course she'd seen trauma before. The rage took over next. She was sick with it.

"Did a boy do that to you?" She was standing suddenly, facing the girl, when she blurted it out. She almost hissed it.

The bruises were fading already, starting to heal. The girl sensed the fear, and a vague warmth moved across her face. "No," she said. And after a moment: "It was a girl."

The two women looked at each other. The creek murmured behind them.

"Why?"

The lanky girl did something very interesting then. Instead of answering she pulled out a cigarette and lit it, lopsided, and through the soft grey smoke she grinned.

Wolfish.

"Well, then," she said, picking up her garbage bag, still empty. "I will get out of your way." The rage was gone from her, understanding. She was falling into thought, and her movements became automatic.

The girl did not say anything as she stepped aside.

She went home, bag empty. Still understanding.

/ / /

She had a glass of red wine on the balcony, remembering the bitter first bite and the slow mellowing after. She missed strange things about her husband now that he was gone; details surfaced and circled down again. She even missed things she didn't know about him and never thought to ask—about himself, as a young man, as a teenager in a purer form. Before work and repetition and time had cast him. Moments were always falling into the next one; moments stumbled over each other until whole weeks and years were gone. He died, his body gave up, and she had missed it. She was working and then she cared for him and then it was over.

But she knew about his heartbreak. He had described it once only as a point on a timeline—married early, she ran off with another man, he didn't marry again until they met decades later. And she already knew that was it. Inside of him there wasn't room for more. She accepted it the way she had accepted her miscarriage, with almost no peace, only the willingness to get through another day to see if it was less tomorrow. And a distant awareness it would never be less.

And they never spoke of it.

Love: the end of a heartbreaking fight for some kind of understanding between strangers. Strangers with an abnormal capacity for hurting each other, all of the unspoken fear around it. Young lovers were so careless and terrified of each other, always, and perhaps that made it exhilarating—but love was the ceasefire.

The girl. Those bruises on her face, they were like her tattoos. The girl wanted them done early; she wanted to learn fast and conquer. Love and sex, jealousy and violence and war, winning and losing. She knew the girl; she knew the young warrior females—even in awkward youth, they were all fire. She herself had been one. She never married until late because she had fire well into her forties. And she suspected her husband had liked women like that—the first wife.

But the girl just didn't know how much life was left, and she wasn't pacing herself. She was rushing, as children do, brave and blind. Into early pain.

RUNNERS

SHE LENGTHENED HER STRIDE IN SLOW SWEEPS, and suddenly a smile moved sideways along her face. She glanced over at me, the smile still on her face but not going to last, then she faced ahead again. It was short but I saw it.

I knew what it was; I loved the moment when running became easy again. It started easy, light on my feet, limbs stretching, weightless on my toes, and thin electric lines starting to move down my legs. But then it would start creeping in eventually—layers of labour and strain. It was ignorable for a while, until my body stopped listening to how I was asking it to move. Heels coming down, heavy, then heavier. Chest turning into a block of wood. But we were all running for the same reason, tied up in everything else: the moment it broke and became easy again. It was such an easy metaphor for everything.

Our group met on Mondays, Wednesdays, and Thursdays; weekends we had off, although many of us would still run, but alone. I ran alone, and I found that I liked that as well—changing routes as the mood took me, taking breaks when I saw something more interesting than cars and houses. Sometimes I stopped in parks and sat under a tree, resting but looking around at the people and children, and then considering other things. The two-hundred-year-old oaks along the edges of the park. Trees were reliable; they reminded you that you weren't going to matter very much. They were calming in that way. Many years before me—or many years after—I could see a kid sitting under those trees, picking up a small fallen branch and breaking off the twigs, one by one, like I would do.

I wasn't a lifelong runner; I ran sometimes for a stretch in my twenties, and then I didn't for a period. Those periods got longer until eventually it just seemed as if I had stopped, and it was final. But Alison died three years ago this past spring, and last year I started up again. I joined the group in May. I didn't know what to expect, socially, but it was an unselfconscious group—no one tried for each other. Pleasantries were brisk and somewhat formal, unenjoyed. I found myself frequently running alongside Sofi, a young woman who preferred running at the back of the pack. It was my preference too, and I studied her sometimes, curious about why she was here. Most of us were decades older.

Sofi must have been in her late twenties or early thirties, white, thin, building up some tough, wiry muscles on her legs now. She put her blonde hair in low ponytails. She had brown roots showing sometimes. Pretty in a standard way, in the way a lot of women were around that age. Richard was probably in his late fifties, stocky, greying but not much, Korean background, some faded acne scars on his cheeks, a younger widower like me. Angela was probably in her fifties like Richard, divorced, sturdy looking, dark-haired, olive-skinned, the mother to four adult children. Angela was probably someone I might have looked at a second time if circumstances were different. Sebastian and Eleanor—you could not have improved the names—were an active, older white couple, freshly retired, freshly tanned, both horse-faced and remarkably fit, as if their entire marriage was based on a variety of fitness activities and strenuous vacations. Climbing things, cycling across something, a boat race where you pedal with your hands. I learned all of this in only one conversation; they did not engage with the rest of us very much—content and whole in their unit. Edward was also retired; formerly an accountant, a Black guy in his sixties, he had a paunch, and his doctor told him to lose it, then his family strongly backed that up. He was losing weight steadily, and I wondered if he would leave the group soon. Katherine may have been the oldest. She was skinny and nearing seventy. She was a widow without children, pale as birch with long white hair she twisted into a bun. And then the inconstant group that sometimes showed up and sometimes didn't: Alex, Jeffrey, Amina, another Katherine who went by Kathy, Winn, and Tony.

I didn't know what to make of Sofi. There was no explanation for why she was with us—she found us online and showed up. Many of us were broken down by one thing or another, illness or grief or aging, loneliness, feeling forgotten by the high buzz of the city belonging to much younger people, caring but also not caring. There was always this thin tension between casual bitterness and not caring. But mostly I saw grief, and bereavement. In brief exchanges you would find out that someone was widowed or freshly divorced—once, a dead child. I didn't want to think about that. Adrienne. She ran down until she must have been barely a hundred pounds, and then she quit. Later I saw her and some weight was back—I thought, it's okay. I thought, she's out. The grief has played out.

My wife was never a runner. It was not how she acquired adrenalin—she loved heights. Her excitement was so complete that she did not even sympathize with people that were afraid of them. "They are afraid because they are asking *what if*. What if I fall. What if the railing breaks. What if I slipped. How can you live like that?" She had very little patience for something perceived as overthinking, an excess of consideration.

In the end it was cancer that took her life. Thirty-two months of pure hell, and then it was over. It took me almost two years to not hate everyone I came across with a violent disgust that twisted my mouth and eyes. And I knew what I looked like—I saw myself once, by accident, in a pane of dark glass. A disgusted old white man staring down a group of teenagers, or couples, or someone with their kids. But they would never know why—and frankly I could not care. For a long time, they didn't even exist.

///

It seems almost unbelievable to me now, but we met on a cruise ship. We were both working there. I went because I had received a pamphlet that listed the four-month seasonal income. She went because she was bored living in a medium-sized town, surrounded by very small towns, anointed with a medium-sized city an hour away. To her, a cruise ship was the moon. It was an entire world away and several spheres beyond.

When you got there, you saw how much the crew was hooking up. Everybody looked you over a few times, men and women. It was a young but haggard working population, serving rotating groups of people who were on their once-in-a-lifetime trip—everybody going nuts—leaving the set-up and clean-up staff with a profound alienation that you could not manufacture anywhere else. Can you imagine—prom for fifty-somethings. For sixty-somethings. Every single night. Something desperate about that bared sunburnt skin, the ecstatic din, the mania and exhaustion, unblinking, the body oils in sharp and synthetic coconut scents, the lineups, the low ceilings. The young staff were unblinking too, faraway and blind to the guests, seeing only each other as fixed points—but those rotated too. Everything was short-term, but time felt long.

I was already a misanthrope—halfway through college and suspecting the outside world was already as I knew it—but that summer it took enormous possession of me. I had been a sullen child and was turning into a sullen young man. I found myself angry not only with individuals but the great mass of us—our smell and our sadness, where and when we thought things could be different for a short while. There were lots of couples among the guests and staff, but it was the loneliest place on earth, a massive white party boat blinking in the middle of a black-blue ocean. The managers there were more like me—living not only with the partiers but the young and rotating seasonal staff. So many people did not come back. The managers who stayed long-term were the kind of people who felt nothing at all.

Alison was a cold slap out of that disaffection, the torpor. She was untouchable. She could climb to any height and remain there, suspended, like a bulb. Her laughter flicking on and off. And that's what she did on the cruise ship, up the antennas so many nights, coaxing me up but giving up on me, sitting up there alone—and then coming down. The job didn't bother her at all—she got what she wanted. Away. She was not bothered by people. But I don't think she necessarily loved them either. She was, always, apart.

///

Sofi Barcette, it said on the email. I found her online. Public, all of her photos, going back years. She looked different early on. Hair light brown, face and cheeks and mouth a little fuller. Now she was thinner but with muscle. Her face was growing more dramatic, arched. Her breasts were flattened into hard semi-circles on her chest. She kept posting photos of herself with words about strength, photos in athletic gear with all the jumpy tendons jutting out of her skin, posture of a fighter. It seemed the new exercise regime meant a lot to her.

It didn't take long to find him. There he was, about two years ago, a guy with a sharp haircut, sharp beard. Handsome, standing tall and with a head-thrown-back contentment. Only one photo left. That one thing we keep after someone has left. I imagine the other photos were incinerated immediately, but this one she could not let go, even publicly—or perhaps especially publicly. She wanted people to know. There were very few photos left from this stretch of time; he must have been in many, all wiped away. The exercise regime started immediately after.

There was a new guy in one or two recent photos. Shorter and stocky, a gym guy, jacked. The rebound.

I had been the rebound twice. First on that cruise ship,

where Alison had come from the Big School Relationship. We parted after the cruise job and met each other again four years later, after an engagement that evaporated. I knew about women that had left lovers, or had had lovers leave them.

/ / /

I had taken a new turn, north through a neighbourhood I didn't know very well. There was already a tug on my right side, close to my ribs, but my legs still felt good. The houses here were smaller and clustered closely together; they were set back further from the sidewalks with long front yards. Behind them, the fenced backyards were short squares. Many lawns were dotted with toys or cheap patio furniture loosely assembled; it was a street where most of life was lived out front. It looked lower income. I slowed and looked around because I wanted to see what it was like.

There was nobody outside because it was a cooler day without much sun. It had rained many hours ago, in the morning. Some front windows showed large televisions, wall-sized, on cartoons or sports or living room comedies. I wished it was warmer out as I walked through the neighbourhood. Still I liked seeing it; at least people still watched television together; at least they were in the same room. That felt like the key detail of a family—being in the same room all the time. In bigger houses everyone was lost in rooms.

There was a small park square with a bench, a garbage can and three trees around it. I sat down with my elbows on my knees, looking down, catching my breath. If you look across the grass, it is green. But if you look down at the grass, you see the green stems standing up, and the layer of yellow and brown underneath. Another metaphor, maybe.

I started to run again as I was turning south. Starting up again was a good feeling, cool legs going warm.

/ / /

I didn't know what to say to Sofi. I felt uncomfortable that I had looked at her pictures, but they were there for everybody to see, her real name. She was proud of all of this—this was her face to the world. Young people were so interested in that.

But I didn't know her at all. I could have been wrong about that guy—maybe he meant nothing; maybe I made assumptions because I had nothing else to do with my time. That's what I had a lot of now—circular time that never moved forward. I didn't actually know anyone anymore.

I wanted to say so much, anyway. I wanted to tell her to stop posting the pictures where she looked strong but it was obvious she was sad and to forget that haircut fucker—leave him behind. I wanted to say he was a mistake that she could not recognize because she couldn't fathom how long the story would actually be and how much would come after. She couldn't see enough because she wasn't at the height yet. I wanted to tell her that nothing was as bad as it seemed—a dark omen because things would inevitably, one day, be a lot worse. One day she would bury someone and live in a dead house and have an endless collection of days to count for nothing and no one. And this guy with the haircut would be little more than an obscene caricature in the empty capitulations of youth.

And when she looked back, she would be ashamed. Not that she would ever actually look back, not to this pointless time—the stubbed toe of a child.

More than that, I wanted to tell her about me and Alison. And what cancer would take away in several meaningless strokes that passed like a season, and how you never had a grip on anything because almost immediately it would change. Pain became an oxygen; you took it in and pushed it out; it kept you alive and awake. Otherwise you were always on the verge of blackout, hovering at the edge of your vision. Good days. They tell you to savour the good days, so I faked it all for her so she would think we were having one—a good day. But there are no good days. There are only days when she is vomiting too much and the following day, when she hardly vomits at all. Was that a good day?

You learned things you never wanted to learn.

I don't know why but I wanted to tell Sofi everything about the past few years, as if she could understand, which of course she could not. But there was an impulse in me. To not let it pass without someone as witness—a particularly unworthy person. A young person with small grievances, too self-conscious, always thinking about how they look. Always presenting. I didn't know why it had to be a person like that. Maybe I had to see for myself how little they cared, like young trees bending in the wind. How little it mattered.

But I never said anything at all. Nothing happened, and we just occasionally ran together at the back of the pack. All of us quietly alone.

/ / /

I started talking to cashiers. Nothing meaningful, but for the first time in my life I would offer something about the weather.

Most grocery stores were staffed with tired, unkempt mothers in their forties and fifties and teen girls there in the short-term. There would be a lull between the beeping scanner and me not having enough to bag yet. "They're calling for rain, but I don't see it," I would say, or some variation, to fill that space.

Most of the women were uncomfortable or bored by that—the older ones would wonder what had happened to me; the younger would assume creepiness. Nothing too alarming, but curious. Once or twice, someone would smile and even say something back. I didn't even reply. I would smile and excuse them back to their world with a downward glance that said I would not intrude again. A small warmth in my throat.

/ / /

When unloading bags, half a dozen oranges spilled hard onto the ground in the parking lot. I had to chase them down, like reckless children, one going under a car. Usually I would be angry, but life had crushed me into a posture of humility—everything was normal now. And I remembered that bruises on a fruit actually turn the fruit sweeter. That was a metaphor too. I had been thinking a lot about metaphors lately and seeing them around me. It was as if the world was trying to show me something.

But pulling out of the lot a few minutes later, I realized that sweetness soon turns to rot. So I didn't like the metaphor anymore. I banished it. It was an Alison thing to do—she felt no shame banishing something of no use to her. She knew almost no shame at all.

Alison had black hair and never dyed it anything else, a kind of arrogance she kept while friends and sisters experimented with colouring their hair in their youth. She had black eyebrows, straight, unarching. Her face was expressive, but she was aloof to many things that would bother me.

She would not have been forgiving of Sofi. Sofi was trying too hard. Nice girl, she would have said at first, but later would slip a comment that showed what she really thought about women like Sofi. The cloying, the asking to be considered, the publicness. Sofi was a pretty, young, professional woman, but still a stumbling calf. Her confidence was patched together with weak things—opinions of others. Alison was a jaguar, creeping along wet green leaves, owing debts only to herself.

As long as she could, Alison was climbing up trees—nimble with practice, if not always fitness—and assuming her rightful perch. Watcher, surveyor with distant eyes. And then teasing, looking down on me.

Cancer decimates everything. No discernment. No selection process. No rightful order. That was the primary break for me—this break between me and the world, even forgiving the fact we never had a strong bond in the first place. A force of nature that could tear down another force of nature; it was a tear within itself. Of all the people in the world—Alison. Arrogant and formidable, crafted by generations of stubborn men and indestructible matriarchs, she was proud of her family. Cancer and Alison were evenly matched. An eighteen-month prognosis went thirty-two months, and I imagine that long deaths are better because we had more time. But I also remember after she died, I slept for days.

When I finally woke, I was blinded by disorientation—profound and narrowing and empty, like a deep cave. And then the grief came in waves, pushing me back. Like I was drowning in there.

Unfairness was something you thought of frequently when your wife was dying. Your home was a hospice now. And when you stepped outside, everything else was the same. So much pathetic human fragility was rotating through your vision—formerly entertaining, now depressing, nothing in between—and yet the one thing you relied upon for being unbreakable suddenly broke. And I had to watch the world continuing around me in mindless rotations, a globe spinning in blue and beige and green—commercials and traffic and an old couple ignoring each other in line. Unfair. Unfair.

You know the dog died, in shock, after Alison? Two days later, just died in her bed.

///

It did reach the point where it became easier for me. I woke up a few minutes before my alarm and sat on the edge of my bed with my feet on the wood floor. I felt like I could run for a long time and that it wouldn't be hard. At my age—I couldn't believe it. My legs came back so quickly, and apparently my lungs had caught up. The other half of the bed was empty. As I stood up, I sensed the mattress adjust. There were odd moments like this—sensations and changes in light and weight and temperature. Strange kitchens, empty sofas. Adjustments concerning the house or furniture.

You read a lot of books and join the groups for people who survive cancer deaths. Grief was a shifting kaleidoscope, absolutely fascinating if your awareness wasn't paralyzed in the moment itself. An art for outsiders. One man kept everything in the house the exact same, quiet as a temple; another man burned books and painted every room; another man sold and moved and worked in a bar in Akron. He did that for two years and then he came back and started a distribution business in restaurant supplies. There were no rules about how to do this. One guy saw handguns wherever he went—sitting on coffee tables and counters, on his desk at work. They were a micro-hallucination for an easy out, a quick exit. They were actually there to comfort him.

I put on my shoes and went for the run, feeling my legs bouncing on elastic springs, ageless, without burden. Anticipating the adrenalin, my lungs shimmered inside my chest as I pulled deep clutches of cool air. When I fell to the back of the pack, Sofi was there, wearing a light coat in the soft blue morning, her legs thin. I was fond of her—the black sheep, a bit sad, a bit brave, despite what Alison might have said. But there was a distance between us that would not allow for a single decent conversation.

Then she surprised me.

"Do you still like running?" she said to me, looking at my face, as we waited to cross a road. "Because I feel like you're flagging."

And she smiled, an effort between strangers.

"I ran before," I said, "but I just started again after my wife, Alison, died."

"Oh, I'm sorry," she said. "I'm sorry."

"It's okay," I said. "It was cancer." My voice was hard on the word.

The light changed and the head of the pack started jogging along and slowly we fell into line behind them. I let myself see a thick slant of early sunlight coming down from the low-rise buildings and casting half of the sidewalk in gold. I felt as if my legs were glowing, yellow-warm.

"I like running," she said. "I like moving."

I didn't respond right away, safe in the movement along the sidewalk and the subtle gathering, dodging, realigning of a group of runners, a flight of birds moving along a city street. I knew this was an opening, but I also knew it would be missed. And yet that was not unsatisfying—it also seemed right.

"Running keeps you busy," I said. It was a boring thing to say and I left the silence to hang, empty, at the end.

"Yeah," she said.

We turned and ran north; I fell behind slightly to give her back her space. Again my mind turned to light and trees and how the world around us was patterned. I thought, Sofi could have taken a picture of all this and posted it, showing all her friends how beautiful it was. But she didn't.

Sofi was ahead of me, taking shorter strides at a tidy pace. She seemed to decide something because she slowed to fall into step beside me.

"Hey," she said.

"Yeah?"

"About two years ago, my mom died." She was looking straight ahead, holding pace. "Got an infection—couldn't fight it out. I don't talk about it, but then..." she trailed off quietly before trying again. "You said your wife—" Her voice caught and stopped.

I didn't say anything at first. My feet moved ahead of each other in a rhythm I knew like breathing. My shoes were white with blue stripes wrapping around the point of the toe, like an arrow. Those bright arrows moved ahead one pace at a time, taking turns, cutting across the grey concrete, swiping through sidewalk squares. I had been relying on that so much—to move time forward, to break out of circular days, seasons, and years.

"I didn't know," I said. It wasn't the right thing to say, but I was realizing I had been wrong—it wasn't the guy with the haircut. It wasn't a child's wounded heart. She was like us, out here; we were all running and running and running. If you don't know what day or month it is, if you can't eat or sleep, but your body still does, dead to itself—you run.

"Of all the people in the world—my mother," Sofi said, not looking at me, red blotches on her face. "No one else was like her. Anywhere. Ever."

"I felt that way too," I said quickly. "Of all people. Alison."

I lost my pace for a few strides, surprised by how surprised I was, how I had relied on our distance. Through her eyes, seeing blindness, how my grief was apart and my own, how it did not matter.

We were running alongside each other, our breath jumping in and out. I thought of Alison and what she would have said of all this—*do what you have to do*.

We caught up to the group at another red light.

"It's true, though," I said. "I'm done." I felt honest. My heart was open and empty.

She turned her head and looked at me. "That's what I thought," she said. "You're done."

Then she surprised me again—a smile, almost a smirk. Brave.

I ran a few more times in the group, and then I went solo, at my own pace, sometimes just walking and sometimes sitting in parks. I sat under trees, never climbed them. Not because Alison had smiled down on me from that height, but because I never knew how.

KIN

1989

SHE WAS AN ANGRY AND EASILY HURT CHILD, face shut up like a fist, mouth snapped up tight. She was nine.

She was taller than most kids, strong, with big arms and pale white legs. She was prone to a sore stomach, afraid to tell her mother and to answer questions about it; she didn't know how to describe it either. It didn't seem to hurt all the time, but when she thought about it, it felt sore.

Every day she walked to school through the damp early morning grass, soothed by how many quiet minutes she had alone between the loud, ugly interiors of her home and the crowded scenes at school. Most of the time, more than anything, she felt bored. She had nine stretches of sidewalk, four lengths of grass, and the counting kept her mind moving forward. The last length was the longest, across the undrawn soccer fields to get to the school—all along the way, lined by small townhouses.

Standing and waiting with the others in gym class, she was too tall, looking down on all of their heads. Most girls fell into semi-formed circles, backs out, while the boys moved in and out of ragged assemblies, restless and loud. At recess she wandered with Amia. She did not like Amia very much, but she was reliably present, hovering by the doors and waiting to walk out together. Amia was ordinary, inside and out. And she knew already that she was not ordinary. She could see it in the way the other girls looked at her—their eyes changed. She was too tall, distracted by strange moods. The boys did not look at her, and she did not look at them.

Amia's hair was a black bowl around her round face. "There's a new boy starting soon," she said plainly. "My brother said."

She wasn't really listening. She was trying to hit a small ball against the ground so it bounced up against the building and returned to her, dutifully. She was trying to find a rhythm with it. She was also counting in her head, although she was beginning to suspect it was not fun anymore—but still she was counting, and she liked ending on fives. Amia was standing off to the side, watching.

She was focused on the satisfying pop-pop of the rubber ball against the concrete ground and the brick wall—and the counting. Ending on a five, taking a short break. Amia didn't say anything else.

A few days later, a thin, strange boy stood at the front of class.

She looked at him, alarmed.

1990

That she could see, Kinn did not talk to anyone at school. Ever. Teachers asked questions of him, and he quietly answered, one word or two, but there was nothing else.

She watched him, carefully, for months. She waited to catch him on a break from his game. She rarely saw him at recess—he went to a hiding spot somewhere or maybe stayed in the school; she could not figure it out. Once in a while, he was outside, wandering around, looking at boys but not going to them.

She wasn't sure why she watched him. She examined the speck of it, carefully, not knowing what it meant. She would turn away, scratching her arm, looking at the rows of houses beyond the loose collection of trees. Then she would turn and look back.

Kinn was slim and dark, with thin arms and legs; he had tight black hair and eyelashes that seemed to flick upward at the corners of his eyes. He was slight but moved slowly, like a much larger animal would. His neck like a deer. The other children streamed through the halls and fields, crowding and dispersing in noisy herds, chasing and laughing. He was a small thing at the edge of her vision at all times—apart, and unwounded by it. Mostly she was curious to watch him start talking, feeling she would notice something that was special. But he held still, and silent.

She hadn't been counting days, but eventually she realized she could recall his first day of school—the day and the month it was. It occurred to her while she was in class, and she waited until she got home to count the days on a calendar, and then she kept the number in her mind, adding one as each day passed. It was her new game.

When he finally spoke, it was on a five.

He walked over to some boys, and they spoke to each other. She was too far away to hear what they said; she stood halfway across the field and froze as if a dark doom was approaching in the sky.

"What is it?" Amia said, pulling her juice box down from her mouth.

She didn't hear the question.

She went home after school and put her bag down on the pile of shoes by the front door, kicking off her own, hurrying to be alone in her room. One of her brothers stopped in the hall, holding a bag of chips and chewing. His hair was lighter than everyone else's in the family, blondish, spiky. He saw where her backpack fell, shouted "Not on my fucking shoes!" and picked up a tissue box from a nearby table. He whipped it at her. The box didn't have enough weight to get close; turning gently in the air, it fell to the ground. Her mother, sitting in the adjoining room, said nothing. She moved her bag roughly, off the shoes, and went upstairs.

She closed the door and crawled onto her bed, turning and lying on her back. Her blood was moving quickly, but when she thought of Kinn it started to slow down. All this time, she could have spoken to him herself—and he would have spoken back. It was curious that she did not think of it before. Now she saw everything within this frame. The dead rabbit she found along the edges of backyards. The neighbour's fat dogs, how it was funny at first, but not later. Her three brothers, mean and loud. She thought of what she could tell him, thinking of the words, choosing them, choosing them again. She wondered what he might say in return.

But in the days and weeks after, she did not speak to him. When he was around, she went into a black mood—grasping at something, becoming angry and silent. She found she could not.

Kinn soon talked to the boys regularly. She watched, not having anything to count, from different parts of the school field.

Amia was drifting away from her, toward other girls, joining the edges of a group with a loud girl in the middle. She noticed it but did not follow. Already the teacher was telling her mother she was different, and she was sensing that other people were noticing and distancing themselves. The empty space around her was growing.

1992

In Grade 7, Kinn stopped talking again.

They had come back from the summer and assembled in restless packs in the same familiar hallways, moving to different rooms. She saw his delicate shoulders, his long neck, his head set slightly forward and always looking in that direction, straight-gazed—she felt again, as she had felt before, that he was older than everyone else. But unhurried. In those loud halls—quiet and potent.

The summer had been a long, bland stretch of time that she did not count until it was closer to the end. Five weeks left, four. She had spent some time in those months reorganizing her closet and refolding her clothes, then watching television into the evening. Her eldest brother was growing quieter, lost in thicker moods, sensing manhood in some of his peers and older boys in the neighbourhood. He ignored her. Her other brothers still sought her out for occasional lashes of cruelty, and she avoided the living room, where they often languished in the heat. At night, she stood in the backyard with her small brown dog wandering around the edge of the fence, sniffing, and waited for him to relieve himself. His name was Pancho. She studied the stars and thought they didn't look real, or at least it didn't seem possible. The summer had passed slowly.

And now, standing in the hallways, lined up to enter a class, she saw the back of Kinn's head—a short patch of white hair dashed across it.

Coming out of classes, slipping by in the halls, she studied him in her distracted, almost angry way—from eye corners, head thrown back as if she did not care. He did not appear at recess; she never knew where he went instead. He did not talk that year.

She would never stop seeking him out, and its meaning was revealing itself to her. She looked around at the pieces of her life and saw only ugly things. Her mother's flat face and wide, heavy build, that early betrayal as a child, slapped and pushed, foul moods, the blank stretches of time when she was ignored and alone. Her brothers and their mindless smashing of toys, their casual abuse, her filthy home. Sitting in the backyard while Pancho walked around the scrubby grass, letting small gravel stones slip slowly through her fingers before picking up another handful. Inside the house, her mother rousing herself to yell at one of her brothers—the effort was becoming rare—the smell of onions frying with salt.

And school—crowded with all the other kids from crowded homes. Everyone loud, clamouring over each other, the humid closeness of them all, pressing up against the glass of her life. Everything else a blind calamity of noise.

Kinn was, at last, a quiet thing.

He did not seem to grow at all. The curve of his brow and cheekbone slipped into the gently upturned jaw, fell into that long neck. Her own big limbs, her own broad, flat face, her tall body—she could not even claim to be like him. Only to be able to see what he was. A delicate animal stepping into a clearing, looking around with ears softly turning.

Late in the year, he was out at recess, walking along the edge of the playground before it became the field, and some boys approached him, loping like ugly dogs. She guessed they would bother him. Two of them did—a remark, some laughter, and more words when he did not respond, then a shove. Like a glass falling and shattering on the ground, her mind split into a thousand directions and her body operated alone, swiftly standing and suddenly breaking across the field. She kicked one boy down from behind before either of them knew what was happening. He fell like a snapped branch. A second boy flew back in shock, his face deformed with fear. But two other boys, shouting, pushed her until she fell, and other children ran at them. The boys kicked at her while she, from the ground, kicked out at them. A shoe struck her jaw, and she whipped her upper body off the ground to save her head. She was still as big as them, and she kicked at a knee, bending it in a direction that it was not supposed to bend, and the shouting turned into a long, horrific shriek that froze everything for three or four blind moments. Teachers were coming. She did not return to school for the rest of the year.

2003

She exited at the rear of the building, near the two loading docks, by the picnic benches, and sat on the concrete stairs. On the leg of one of the picnic benches it was carved into the wood:

only poor boys
give good head

She looked at it often because it was so many letters and not so poorly done. Someone had spent time.

She pulled out a cigarette and lit it, replacing the lighter in her pocket. She tried to understand it—not as a vulgar thing, but as something to know about men. She had known poor boys, turning into young men in the clumps of housing where she grew up. Belonging, and not. Growing up aching and not knowing why, leaving school for work, putting all their money into a car, good shoes, and smoking up. Getting lonely in the evenings. Does that type of man give better head? Boys in nice houses, in sports and camps, bookshelves filled with things—they don't get on their knees? She thought it might be true. She saw the words several times a day, smoking at the back of the building, once or twice before lunch, once or twice after.

Of course it hadn't been true for her. She tried a young man once, but it was all wrong. He was not serious; she was too serious. Hurrying, he pulled down his pants to reveal red boxers covered in yellow smiley faces—she stopped everything and stared at them. Her pride stung her, a great wound in whatever she was attempting. She knew her body: out of the shower, pale and gleaming, this formidable thing. Her shoulders were set back, locked in defiance; she could run without tiring on legs of incredible power. That she should undress for the red boxers with yellow faces was pathetic—he was absurd, a peasant. It was over.

For a long time she had not even known she was poor. Growing up everybody was, and so she didn't suffer for it. If you had heat in winter and ate every day, you were every other kid. Her mother was homebound and couldn't drive, so they never left the neighbourhood; they took a short bus for food. But her brothers started driving and later, when she was a teenager, taught her. She got a high school job and spent years in a cheap, shuddering car, driving across the city and dropping into small plazas along the highway. Cruising through other areas, going downtown, passing gleaming cars with silent children in the backseat and two well-groomed parents up front, seeing other teenagers from other parts of town, their later models glittering. Only seeing all this did she know she was poor. She sensed that she was to submit to it: the humility of it, the lowered position. But she couldn't. And she didn't.

Driving through her neighbourhood, she saw packs of young men in strip plazas, leaning on their cars, white shoes glowing, wolf heads hanging low on their shoulders. Watching her pass. Thousands in rims but still living at home—crashing with half-girlfriends in basement apartments. Living a half-life while waiting for something better.

Stopped at red lights, she would turn and meet their eyes.

She had dropped out of school in twelfth grade and went full-time at a restaurant, first in the kitchen and then serving during the dinner rush. They moved her to grill after a while, gave her a raise. But she was bored. She finished her GED over a summer and got a job with a good company in manufacturing, packing boxes and checking orders. Later, after a year of that, they promoted her to supervisor—the last supervisor got pregnant with her third child and wasn't going to come back. She was making good money now and barely twenty, checking orders from a desk and occasionally helping other teams. She had money, more than enough. She still liked to count sometimes, ticking things along her fingertips, up to five, then starting again. She went to work every day with a sense of duty and the details of it didn't matter. But the truth was, she was bored—a final thing, settling in her bones.

Kinn had died before she dropped out, late in eleventh grade. They had announced it solemnly at school: *Our classmate has passed away*. There was a photo of him in a frame standing upright that the teacher had pulled from a wrinkled plastic bag at the bottom of her desk. The students listened at first but eventually grew restless at the back. She heard chatter in the desks behind her; a pen dropped to the floor. A chair scraped under the heavy lean of somebody picking it up. The teacher was talking. He had a condition and was in the hospital for much of that year; he'd had the condition his whole life. A girl muffled a sneeze. The teacher struggled to pronounce the medical term with three long words but said it was always fatal. Words blurred out. The talk behind her fell away as she seemed to be standing quite separate now, somewhere out of the room—a thickly silent place where she couldn't remember anything else from that day. She remembered, outside the windows, it was spring, yellow and green.

It seemed Kinn had known all along. That fact stayed with her. She decided then that everyone was dying but not everyone knew it; most people pushed it to the back, but a few people held it at the front. She never spoke of him, not once, to anybody, in all those years.

Sometimes, she saw Kinn in others.

She could see him in children when they were still young and wandering—delicate things, before they started clamouring amongst themselves. Once she saw him in twin sisters sitting side-by-side on the bus, girls with long black hair in single braids, long necks with chins lifted. It was rare she saw children ten or eleven years old sitting quietly like that, hands resting in their laps, gazing out the windows with such calm consideration. It was rare she saw anyone. They stood up to leave the bus in such sweet and simple movements, careless and elegant—twins from a strange dream. Like a sign. And she remembered Kinn's languid movements as he walked or slowly turned his head. A smooth, sensitive animal—vulnerable, but without fear.

All of her brothers had disappeared. They got jobs and left the house, sending her mother, on disability, some money sometimes. She stayed home with their mother and paid a small rent, and they mostly stayed in different parts of the house.

She was at the grocery store on a Wednesday night, buying heartburn pills for her mother and picking up a pack of cigarettes for herself to save the morning trip. A man was watching her. She looked at him for a few moments and felt a subtle movement beneath the ground, a shift in her understanding. A deep memory rose in her.

It was Kinn's older brother.

He was older, thicker, darker, with a heavy beard that was cropped close to his face. He was staring at her, recognizing her, recalling images. She looked back and did the same. He remembered her from school: the girl who got in trouble, who got mad, the loner in the shadows. Got in a fight over Kinn. She could not remember anything about him, but she saw the likeness and remembered his presence, distant, somewhere at the edge of things.

She realized a few things very quickly. He likely still lived in the area. He was curious about her. He would come back again and try to talk to her.

2004

She was, ultimately, a shy thing. Easily wounded but strong-hearted, willing to defend herself. That was the part that no one understood about her, that she barely understood about herself—how the anger was frustration, the mute wall she had built around herself, the height and distance that deprived her of air. But she was also saving herself. Without the wall, she would be exposed and bare, struck by so much blunt indifference. Like body blows.

She could never handle people's casual relationships, especially with important things. People let beauty and meaning pass them by. Everyone was dying but pretended they weren't. Disinterest. Indifference. She took little offence to actual insult but felt brutalized by people who didn't care—and there were so many.

"Birchmount Park?"

She had avoided the grocery store for almost six months but later trickled back, it being on her way home from work. She went on odd weeknights—Tuesdays, Mondays—rather than late in the week when most people went. The truth was, she was scared to see him again. That day something had leapt out of her—a wild terror—and silently immolated itself.

It had rained in the early evening and the streets were still wet, glowing with pink and yellow strips of lights from cars. She was feeling young lately, simple-hearted. She was putting more money into her car, paying for cleanings and upgrading her sound system for the second time. She was going to the grocery store to get ice cream and got about halfway through an aisle before she recognized him, in profile, standing close to the end. He looked up and saw her.

He asked about Birchmount Park, and she said yes. She looked at him without emotion; he was animated.

"Yeah, I remember you," he said.

"You're Kinn's brother?" she asked. She wanted to say his name.

He hesitated for a short moment. "Yeah," he said.

They talked for a few minutes, and she could read the simple messages that showed in men's faces when they were not prepared. *Hello, hello, hello, hello.* He seemed to grow taller as they spoke, smiling easily and warmly. But she already saw that he was not Kinn; he didn't even understand how his brother was different, an elegant shadow on a cave wall. He was ordinary and—its primary characteristic—did not know it.

Her own heart fell in slow, heavy thumps against her ribs, again and again, like a failing heartbeat.

She forgot the ice cream and left the store after their chat ended. She went home, parking briskly in the narrow driveway between their small house and the multiplex next door. When she went into the house, her mother rustled in the other room but did not speak or come out, so she did not say anything either. Her mother had started smoking again; she could smell fresh smoke. She coughed through the days and nights. The walls in her home were darkly painted and she felt, as she always had, her whole life, that the house was suffocating.

She went straight upstairs and into her own small living room, finding the bottle of rye and the shot glass on her shelf, taking one quick shot and then a second. She felt better after that, more even. Kinn was dead, and she had no recourse for that. Her predicament now was the life she had left—long, missing things most people did not even notice. She went back downstairs quietly and slipped into her mother's bedroom, into the closet, rummaging briskly for the wooden box that had been there since she was a girl, left behind from her mother's old boyfriend—a small, black revolver. She held her breath and checked—still loaded. She was moving quickly now, less concerned with making noise and more focused on everything happening fast. She briefly thought of returning upstairs, but instead sat on her mother's bed and held up her left hand, pressing the barrel into her palm and, after quickly glancing up at the ceiling and then back down, shot straight through the middle of her hand.

Pain tore through her mind, a jagged red crack split open behind her eyes. Her mouth opened but made no sound. Her lungs clawed for air.

Her mother let out a sharp cry from the next room.

Her hand was covered in blood. She lowered the gun, pressed it against her wrist, and shot again.

2006

She lost the hand. They told everyone it was an accident, but two accidental shots did not make sense, so she was assigned a psychiatrist and the police took away the gun. It was all right; she was finished.

She saw the psychiatrist. She already knew about the personality and learning disorders; she had seen a doctor in high school. She didn't much feel like describing how she didn't love anything or anyone, or the boredom, or being asexual, or a dead boy, and she didn't see how medication would change that. The doctor wanted to talk about her mother or brothers, but they did not interest her. She tried the pills anyway for a few months to see if it would be different this time—it wasn't. She threw the bottle out. She was able to keep her job with limited duties and could still drive. Within a year and a half, not so much had changed.

She saw the psychiatrist a couple more times after that. He was a thin man, old, with round glasses, and always wearing corduroy pants that were fading badly around the knee. She thought he was exactly as a doctor would be described in a book. But he was nice, and she didn't mind talking about her dog with him; she seemed to have a lot of memories about the dog.

She took two things from him and kept them close. He once called her a protector—of what, she never knew—but still it rang, painful, like a bell in her chest. And he had framed quotes on his wall. One of them said, *Learn to walk in the sweetness of the possession of your own soul.* That one rang for a long time.

She was leaving the grocery store and there he was again, Kinn's older brother, looking after her. But now he did not come to talk to her. She struggled with her bags, slinging them onto her left forearm, missing its hand—the cashier looked away with colour rising in her face. She knew he was watching. She started to walk out of the store, slower than she needed to, making a fuss with the bags in the crook of her elbow, as if she struggled with it. She was showing him something; she wanted him to see. And she felt suddenly light.

ACKNOWLEDGEMENTS

All my gratitude to the same people as my first book. New joiners: Kim, tasked with the copyedit, saving me from myself, patient collector of my mistakes. Bryan, my editor for this collection, careful and wise, salty and true, your favourite stories were my favourite too. A kinship. Megan, your art is a gift. And Nick, my university reward, egregiously overlooked earlier, but you forgave me, as kind as you've been all these years. My SP family, I miss you. As before: Akin, you found me. Norm, you chose me. I owe so much to you both. Outside of this world, you are still my favourite people. And Douglas, thank you for telling me to write.

NINA DUNIC is a two-time winner of the *Toronto Star* Short Story Contest, has been longlisted by the CBC Short Story Prize four times, and was nominated for The Journey Prize. CBC Books named her in its 2023 Writers to Watch list. Her debut novel *The Clarion* won the 2024 Trillium Book Award, was longlisted for the 2023 Giller Prize, was selected as the Best Canadian Debut by Apple Books, and was a *Globe and Mail* Best Book of 2023. Nina lives in Scarborough, ON. Find out more at ninadunic.com.

Invisible Publishing produces fine Canadian literature for those who enjoy such things. As an independent, not-for-profit publisher, we work to build communities that sustain and encourage engaging, literary, and current writing.

Invisible Publishing has been in operation for nearly two decades. We released our first fiction titles in the spring of 2007, and our catalogue has come to include works of graphic fiction and nonfiction, pop culture biographies, experimental poetry, and prose.

We are committed to publishing writers with diverse perspectives. In acknowledging historical and systemic barriers, and the limits of our existing catalogue, we emphatically encourage writers from LGBTQ2SIA+ communities, Indigenous writers, and writers of colour to submit their work.

Invisible Publishing is also home to the Bibliophonic series of music books and the Throwback series of CanLit reissues.